THE OMEGA STRAIN

MITCH HERRON 1

STEVE P. VINCENT

For Joan McCay. Forever in my memories.

1

"138."

Mitch Herron's voice was a whisper on the wind as his target's blood sprayed the forest floor and his camouflaged body dropped to the ground.

Herron scanned the outskirts of the woods, searching for his next kill. The dense terrain sloped away from him, the trees thinning gradually the closer they got to the compound that housed his targets. He'd scouted the forest and outskirts of the compound, so he knew exactly where his prey would be found.

Forty seconds later – right on schedule – he spotted the final sentry walking through the trees, cradling a shotgun and chewing on tobacco. He stopped to spit and Herron fired a short burst from his silenced submachine gun. Each shot made a sound like a nail gun and the guard dropped, leaving a spray of pink mist in his wake. With the last sentry down the compound was exposed to predators.

Predators like Herron.

"139." He added the dead man to his tally, a career's worth of corpses he'd left littered behind him. The number would grow before the night was done.

Death was Herron's business and business was good. He was a scalpel, used by the U.S. Government to slice out cancers like these fanatics. Four days from now, on World Environment Day, they planned to unleash a biological weapon. U.S. Government assets had validated the threat and passed the job over to Herron's handler with full clearance to wipe the fanatics out.

There were six more to go.

Herron stalked toward the compound, using the forest and shadow to mask his movements, and stopped at the tree line. The compound was made up of four square buildings, cheaply built in the middle of nowhere and with no security except for the guards. The fanatics were relying on their isolation to keep them safe. That mistake would cost them everything.

Herron spotted his next victim on a path that skirted the perimeter of the compound, only a few yards from the forest's edge. Whereas the guards had been heavily camouflaged, this man wore casual clothes and strolled unarmed, smoking a cigarette. The forest and the compound were almost silent, but Herron was confident he'd be able to sneak up behind the man without making a sound. He let his SMG hang from its strap, drew his combat knife and moved in.

When he was close enough, he struck in one explosive motion, placing his left hand over the man's mouth and pulling his head closer. Simultaneously, he thrust the point of the blade into the base of his skull. The knife severed the man's spinal cord, causing an immediate loss of primary body functions — breathing and heartbeat.

Herron pulled the man's head back and ran the blade across his throat. Blood sprayed the path and Herron heard the last air he'd ever breathe escape from his severed windpipe. In two swift strikes, Herron had rendered his body useless — unable to function or warn others. Herron let go of the man and he flopped to the ground. He'd be dead in seconds.

140.

He didn't bother hiding the body. There was too much blood for that. Instead, he continued through the compound to deal quickly with the five remaining targets. He sheathed his knife, gripped the SMG and made for the nearest wall. He inched along it, paused when he reached the end and peeked around the corner. A man was leaning against the wall about halfway down its length.

Herron took a second to scan his broader surroundings. The compound was large and sparsely populated. There was no one else around, and the only sound Herron could hear was the man as he whistled softly to himself. He was good to go. After a deep breath, he turned the corner, aimed his weapon at the man's head and fired a quick burst. The target got a few rounds between the eyes and dropped.

141.

Herron kept the SMG raised as he moved in to confirm his target was dead. While the SMG was relatively quiet, the trade-off was that it fired small caliber rounds that didn't always kill. He kicked the man to confirm it – he was a lifeless hunk of meat – then, after taking a second to swap out his magazine, Herron prepared to move again.

"Haven't you caused enough trouble?"

The voice surprised Herron and he turned, his SMG searching for the speaker. Two shotguns were pointing at him, held by separate assailants – one wearing a suit and the other a giant of a man. Though he'd been almost silent, they'd somehow been alerted to his presence. Herron considered firing, but from this range the shotguns would tear him in half. The odds were abysmal.

"Drop your weapon." It was the same man who'd spoken before. The shotgun he was sporting was at odds with his well-cut suit. "I won't ask twice."

Herron tossed the SMG on the ground. Then he felt a flash of pain and everything went black.

* * *

"Oomph." The blow to his stomach forced all the air from Herron's lungs. He coughed and grimaced. "About time you guys showed up."

Nobody answered and all he could hear was footsteps. The hood over his head prevented him from seeing anything and he couldn't move. His captors had sat him in a chair and cable-tied his wrists to its armrests and his ankles to its legs. Worse, a thick rope had been cinched around his waist and he had a splitting headache from where he'd been hit on the back of the skull.

All up, his day had gone to shit.

"What now?" Herron coughed one more time. "I'm not a bad guy, you know? Can't we just talk about this?"

He could have been blindfolded for hours for all he knew, halfway between asleep and awake. While he needed to stay alert, his body wanted the opposite, so he'd been forced to use all his best tricks to stay awake. In his head, he'd counted to a thousand, run through the steps to clean all his favorite weapons and ranked his favorite sexual partners. Then he'd done it all again in reverse.

All the while, the deadline for the release of the fanatics' pandemic drew closer. By now they'd have found the bodies of the dead sentries. They were seven men down, but Herron doubted that would compromise their agenda enough to stop them. All he'd achieved was to warn them that the authorities knew about their plan.

The hood was pulled from his head and

Herron's eyes were flooded with searing light that forced them closed. He opened them again, blinking rapidly to adjust. The same fanatics who'd captured him stood in front of him. One was the mountain of a man, equal parts fat and muscle, while the other was the suited man who'd spoken to him earlier. He worried Herron more than the brute.

Herron's surroundings were much as he would have predicted – a concrete floor and plaster walls with no decoration or distinguishing features. The only things in the room were the chair Herron was sitting on and a small table off to the side with a cloth covering it. This wasn't a hardened room designed to hold captives, it was a storage room that had been converted into a makeshift jail.

Hopefully, his jailers were as amateur as their jail.

Herron ignored the brute and looked straight at the suited man, sure he was the fanatic leader. "Mike Freeman, I assume?"

"You got me. And quite a few of my men, it seems." Amusement twinkled in Freeman's eyes. He was smug, thought he'd won. "Care to tell me who you are?"

Herron didn't respond. Eventually Freeman sighed and the brute stepped forward, fist cocked to strike. This time, Herron was ready and braced his body as the blow landed on his chin. It rattled him but didn't have the same impact as the first shot he'd taken. The large man grunted, dissatisfied, and prepared for another shot at him.

Freeman cleared his throat. The man-mountain turned to face him and Freeman shook his head. "Leave him."

Herron hocked and spat blood on the floor, never taking his eyes off Freeman. "You're wasting everyone's time."

"You got somewhere better to be?" Freeman scoffed. "I want to know who you are and who sent you."

"There's a lot of things I'd like to know, too." Herron gave a grim smile. "Starting with which of you would prefer to die first."

The thug snarled and started forward, but Freeman held out a hand and ordered him back, a tiny smile creasing the edge of his mouth. Herron had hoped to get them angry and force a mistake, knowing it was the easiest way to get free, but clearly Freeman was too smart for that. The fanatic leader wasn't in the mistake business.

"You're full of pep, aren't you?" Freeman leaned in close to Herron. "You've done nothing to compromise our years of work. None of the damage you've done will be lasting."

Herron shrugged as much as his restraints would allow. "Why World Environment Day? Surely there are more worthy occasions?"

Freeman seemed slightly taken aback that Herron knew the date of release, but the brief flash of shock was quickly covered over. "None more perfect for making humanity pay for the environmental destruction it has wrought or restoring balance to the planet. Now, let's try again. Who're you?"

"Daenerys of the House Targaryen, the First of Her Name, The Unburnt, Queen of the Andals, the Rhoynar and the First Men..." Herron spat more blood. "Want me to continue?"

Freeman sighed and walked over to the table against the wall. He removed the cloth that was covering it, revealing a basic set of torture objects — kitchen knives and garage tools. Herron almost laughed at the thought of him raiding kitchen drawers and tool boxes to find some items for his hulk to work with. Almost. Even basic tools could damage the human body. It didn't even take much skill.

"Last chance." Freeman raised an eyebrow. "The easy way or the hard way?"

"My mother told me never to trust anyone who took the easy way out." Herron smiled.

"Suit yourself. Tell my man when you're ready to talk." Freeman exited the makeshift prison without looking back.

"Just you and me, big guy." Herron locked his eyes on the brute. "Let's see if you've got enough muscles and brains to get what you need."

* * *

Herron clenched his teeth so hard his jaw hurt, adding to his pounding headache. He tried to keep silent as his torturer attacked his left thumbnail with a pair of pliers, but a guttural growl eventually escaped his throat. The ogre pulled and fire burned through Herron's hand as the nail finally popped loose. He closed his eyes and rode out the pain, just as he'd done several times over the last few hours.

When he opened his eyes again, the brute was holding his thumbnail up as a trophy, using the pliers to rotate it so they could both see. The big man smiled, the first sign of emotion Herron had seen from him. He hadn't said a word, no matter how much Herron tried to coax a reaction out of him, to prompt a mistake or a human interaction that he could exploit.

"Harder than in the movies, isn't it?" Herron smiled, teeth bloody from the repeated head shots he'd taken. "I'll save myself the trouble when it's my turn and take your fingers off with bolt cutters."

The towering sadist didn't respond, just tossed the pliers back onto the table and perused his collection of rudimentary torture implements. It only took him a second to pick up the same long chef's knife that he'd used several times before. Despite the pain he'd suffered, Herron knew it could be worse. His captor was either incompetent or holding back.

His torturer moved closer, bringing the blade slowly towards Herron's cheek. Herron sat up straight in the chair and smiled. If he were doing the torturing, he'd have taken a hammer to every movable joint and then used the knife to work on the extremities and squishy bits — toes, fingers, penis, eyes, tongue. He was glad he hadn't received that sort of treatment yet.

Herron gritted his teeth again as the blade sliced his right cheek, adding more blood to the slick already covering his face, his naked torso and the floor. He'd tried threatening the thug with no effect, so it was time to press another button. As soon as the cutting stopped, he spoke.

"Is this the best you can do? Did Freeman order you to keep me alive or are you too stupid to know where to cut?"

The brute's eyes flashed and Herron knew he'd hit a nerve. Stepping back, the gorilla shifted his grip so that the blade was facing down and raised the weapon to strike. Herron braced for the blow as the knife flashed down.

"Enough!"

The shouted order was too late to stop the brute, but in time to ensure he pulled the blow. The blade bit into Herron's thigh, but not as deeply as it might have done. The pain was still immense and Herron cried out, throwing curses at his torturer.

Freeman stepped into the room and placed a hand on his enforcer's shoulder, but his eyes were locked onto Herron. . The big man rubbed a hand over his face.

"What'd you say to Copernicus to get him so angry?" Freeman's eyes twinkled in curiosity.

"Copernicus?" Herron gritted his teeth against the pain.

Freeman smiled thinly and turned to the brute.

"Has he said he's willing to talk yet?"

Copernicus shook his head.

Freeman sighed and reached into his pocket for a small, plastic container about the size of a spectacles case. He opened it to reveal a syringe and a small glass vial of clear liquid. Herron's eyes widened. He could recover from a beating and some cuts, but the mystery substance was far more concerning. Freeman removed both items from the case, penetrated the vial with the syringe and drew back on the plunger.

Freeman put the case on the table and held up the syringe for Herron to see. "Are you going to stop wasting my time?"

Herron shrugged. "I have a cover story, but we both know it's bullshit. All I'm prepared to tell you is that I'm going to shove that case up your ass."

Freeman smiled and gestured Copernicus in Herron's direction. The goon moved toward the chair and clamped his hands down on Herron's right arm, pinning it in place. Herron struggled, but it was futile. Freeman stalked closer with the syringe, his evil smile broadening. Having people under his control was clearly something he enjoyed.

"There's no use resisting." Freeman slipped the needle into Herron's arm and pressed down on the plunger. "There."

"What the fuck did you just put in me?" Herron shouted.

"Oh, you'll find out." Freeman stepped back and nodded at Copernicus. "Leave him and the other prisoner. The rest of us are leaving. You clean up and follow as soon as you can."

Herron's ears pricked up. *The other prisoner?*

Copernicus nodded and began whistling a tune as Freeman left the room. The big man returned to the table, covered the torture implements with the cloth and placed the hood over Herron's head. A second later, the sound of his retreating footsteps seemed to confirm that the torture was at an end. Though he was glad the pain would stop, Herron was far more worried about whatever Freeman had jabbed in him and that his mission hadn't been completed.

Herron had failed.

2

HERRON LISTENED for the sound of Copernicus returning but there was only silence. He started to rock back and forth on the chair and it took only a few moments to build enough momentum to topple it. As he fell back, he kept his head forward and tensed his core. The chair struck the ground, Herron grunted in pain and then smiled. The right arm of the old wooden chair had come away with the impact. Though it was still cable-tied to his wrist and the other arm of the chair remained connected to the frame, the fall had done the seat enough damage to give Herron a chance.

It was still going to be a pain in the ass to get free, though.

He struggled over to the table in a crouching wriggle, dragging the detritus of the chair in his wake, and removed the cloth covering Copernicus's tools. Some of the implements were slicked with his blood, but Herron's mind was focused on one simple task: finding a tool to cut the cable ties. He settled on the pliers that had removed his thumbnail, which also had a wire cutter. As he started, from outside came the rumble of several engines starting. Herron paused to listen. It sounded like...

Are they leaving?

Herron raced to cut himself loose from the remains of the chair, before he lost his targets forever. He had to force himself to concentrate, but it didn't take long. At last, when his four limbs were free of the cable ties, he used the chef's knife to cut through the rope that bound his waist to the chair.

He took a second to assess his injuries: he had a pounding headache, a deep cut in his thigh, some smaller cuts, a missing thumbnail and a lot of bruises.

Taking a knife to the cloth from the table, he cut one thin strip and one larger section, which he folded into a makeshift pad for the deep cut on his thigh. He placed the pad over the wound, wrapped the thinner strip of cloth around his thigh and tied it tightly. It wasn't pretty but it would stop the bleeding and keep him going.

Herron gripped the knife and slipped from his cell. As he'd suspected, it was simply an empty room in a compound not filled with crazies. He walked gingerly down the corridor, limping from the cut in his thigh and sore from his beating. The other rooms in this building were similarly empty, so he made for the heavy steel door that led outside.

It was dark and as best Herron could figure it was the early hours of the morning. The compound was deserted. Everyone really had gone, with the possible exception of Copernicus and the second prisoner Freeman had referred to. His overriding goal now was to find information that would tell him where the fanatics were going.

The compound had four buildings, counting the empty one he'd just left. Made of gray concrete, with no decoration or adornment, they were laid out in a two-by-two square. Each had a single door inside, the perfect spot for an ambush, but Herron was relaxed given Copernicus was the only one who might be left to spring it.

The second of the four buildings was unused, like the first, presumably to provide plenty of space the fanatics could expand into if they wanted. Outside of it he found dozens of steel military-style gas cans filled to the brim with far more gas than the fanatics would need to keep their vehicles topped up, but Herron ignored them and kept moving.

The third building was Freeman's quarters – just one large room, furnished on the cheap. It was cluttered and Herron wondered why Freeman had just abandoned it. Perhaps that's why he'd told Copernicus to clean up. Herron made his way through the room, emptying drawers and upending furniture until he came to a large hardwood desk. The drawer was locked.

Hoping it was sturdy enough, Herron slipped the blade of the kitchen knife into the gap and forced the lock. It gave with a splintering crunch. Inside the drawer, he found all that remained of his gear – his combat knife and his bump keys, which would cater to most any lock he cared to try. Herron pocketed them and tossed the kitchen knife onto the floor, preferring his own blade. Herron also pocketed a screwdriver and wad of cash, figuring both might be useful.

Most interesting of all the drawer's contents was a manila folder stuffed full of paper files. A flick through the papers revealed a list of names, which might well be a list of the fanatics. The rest of the files were a mystery to him, because he couldn't make sense of chemical formulas and research reports. From what he could understand, it was almost certain that the folder contained some of the answers he needed.

He'd found a lead. He smiled. "Jackpot."

Herron searched the office for something to carry the files and settled on a small backpack. A moment after he'd stuffed them inside, he heard a woman scream from somewhere nearby. Herron's cheer was doused like a candle hit by a firehose. It had to be the other prisoner. And if she was screaming, it was a safe bet it was Copernicus.

Herron was keen to resume their chat. Once again, he was the predator.

* * *

Herron didn't have to look far for answers – a whimpering noise from behind a closed door soon told him he'd found the right place. With the screwdriver in one hand and the knife in the other, he eased the door open. The source of the whimpering was a woman, half undressed and cowering as Copernicus stood over her, brandishing a cleaver.

"Decided on a little recreation?" Herron smiled as Copernicus spun towards him. "Everyone else has gone without you."

Confusion and anger flashed across the brute's face. "How—"

"He speaks!" Herron laughed and changed his grip on the knife, so that he was holding it underhand. "You should have left with the others."

Herron looked down at the woman. She was a mess. Near her, two of the military gas cans stood in the corner. His eyes widened. Copernicus hadn't just been tasked with cleaning up the compound. He'd planned to use the gas inside the cans to burn the place to the ground.

Herron stalked forward, knife ready. Copernicus tensed and gripped the cleaver tighter; he moved slowly, but with his hips, which meant his strikes would be powerful. It didn't matter that Herron was skilled. All it would take was a lucky cut to an artery and he'd be finished. He needed to be careful.

In the movies, someone with a knife would wave it around, slashing at the target's body of a target and giving them the chance to react, but Herron knew better. His knife sliced straight at the brute's neck, aiming for the artery. Copernicus held his hands up to defend his neck.

It gave Herron the opening he'd wanted.

With his left hand, Herron thrust the concealed screwdriver into the giant's side, piercing the bigger man's body. Herron landed three quick strikes before he could react, piercing his stomach and leaving him open for an attack with Herron's right hand. He stabbed at the artery in the brute's neck.

"Had enough?" Herron retreated as blood spewed from the brute's artery. The last thing he wanted was blood in the eye.

The other man howled in pain and took a swing. In his weakened state, Herron was moving a split-second too slow and it rang his bell. He stumbled to one knee. Needing to take down Copernicus for good, he reached around the back his feet and slashed at his left Achilles tendon.

The other man let out a blood-curdling howl as his left leg buckled and he fell. Herron climbed to his feet, knowing it was over. The other man gripped his neck, trying to stop the bleeding. It was hopeless. Blood spewed between his trembling fingers and he stopped moving.

"142." Herron stared at the brute a second, then switched his attention back to the woman.

She was crying, her eyes on his knife as she sobbed, "Please, don't hurt me!"

He looked at her with hard eyes. She was obviously the other prisoner. She clutched the shreds of her t-shirt over her bra and chest. "Who are you and why are you here?"

Another sob escaped her throat, but she was fighting hard to regain some composure. She climbed unsteadily to her feet and stood face-to-face with him, a posture that seemed important to her but was utterly meaningless to him.

"I'm Erica Kearns." Her voice wavered as she pushed her tangled mess of hair behind her ears. "They kidnapped me."

"Why?"

"I work for the CDC, I'm a specialist in highly contagious pathogens and synthetic, slow acting viruses. They snatched me from my home and forced me to run tests on a virus."

Herron tensed. "What kind of tests?"

"They demanded I look at a small part of the virus' biological makeup. I never got to see the whole thing, but what they did show me was synthetic. They wanted me to confirm it would act slowly. I told them it would and they left me to rot. Until…"

"Until Romeo here showed up." Herron glanced down at Copernicus, then looked back at Kearns. "Did you ever meet their leader?"

"No."

Herron removed his backpack, pulled out the folder he'd found and handed it to her. "What do you make of this?"

She took the papers and started to flick through them, her brow creased in concentration. "This is a lot more than they showed me before."

Herron asked a question that'd determine whether he left her here or took her with him. "These guys injected me with something. Can you tell me what it is?"

"Maybe. There might be a record in here. Or, failing that, if I can get you to a lab I can run a few tests and..." Her voice trailed off. She was looking at the piece of paper in her hand like it was a bomb.

"What is it?"

"It can't be." She looked up at him. The color had drained from her face. Then she looked back at the paper. "It's just an urban legend."

"What is?"

"The Omega Strain."

"What's that?" Herron asked, impatient. "I don't speak Greek."

"It might well mean the end of the world."

* * *

Herron coaxed every ounce of performance out of the old Chevrolet sedan as he steered down the rural roads away from the fanatics' Georgia compound. He and Kearns had pilfered fresh clothes from the gear the fanatics had abandoned in the rush to leave, then he'd used his bump keys to steal the car. Now they were speeding towards the CDC in Atlanta to get some answers, and the sense of purpose should have made Herron feel better. Instead, he couldn't shake the bitter taste of failure.

At last Kearns broke the silence. "So, what's your name? I don't usually climb into cars with strange men."

Herron took his eyes off the road for only a second to glance at her. He didn't like company and was already wondering if bringing her along was the right decision. "Mitch."

"Mitch... You don't seem like a Mitch to me. What's your full name?"

"Just Mitch." Herron shut down that line of questioning before it really got started. "Tell me more about the Omega Strain."

"It's a CDC urban legend, a viral pathogen that makes Ebola look like a head cold. If it's real, though..."

Herron nodded. The implications were clear, though he didn't understand the science. That was the only reason Kearns was sitting in the passenger seat. He preferred working alone, but without Kearns he'd have no clue about what to do next. He didn't know where the fanatics had gone, how they were planning to release their virus, what the virus was and what the substance was inside him. The only thing he knew was that in three days, on World Environment Day, it would be too late. Having Kearns along for the ride at least gave him the chance to answer some of those questions.

"Your lab at the CDC... you think they might be able to figure out what's inside me?"

"Maybe, I..." She paused, clearly thinking better of whatever she was going to say.

"What?" Herron's eyes narrowed.

"Nothing." She yawned and closed her eyes.

Herron was tired himself, but he had no time to rest. If Kearns wasn't going to give him any answers until they reached Atlanta, he'd just have to get them there as fast as he could. After that, he could ditch her. He shuffled in his seat and got comfortable for the long drive ahead. Or as comfortable as he could be with multiple wounds, anyway.

Four hours out from Atlanta, the fuel light flashed red. By then the morning sun was bright and Herron had long since got them onto a highway, so he knew it wouldn't be too hard to find a gas station. Sure enough, he soon spotted a small station up ahead – just two pumps and a convenience store, but it was open. He pulled in and brought the car to a stop.

Herron cleared his throat loudly and Kearns was roused from sleep. "We're stopping for five. Use the bathroom if you need to."

He didn't wait for her to respond. He took coins from the console, opened the door and got out. As he pumped the gas, he watched Kearns through the window. She stretched out full in her seat and tied her brown hair into a mess of a ponytail, before she too climbed out of the car.

"Pay for the gas and get us some supplies." Herron dug through his pocket and fished out a small wad of bills. "High-calorie junk food and some water."

Her eyes still heavy with sleep, she shrugged, took the cash and then moved in the direction of the convenience store. A moment later Herron finished filling the car and placed the gas pump back in its cradle. He'd spotted a pay phone near the road as he'd pulled in and now he wandered over to it and inserted some coins. The number he dialed he knew by memory.

The call connected and Herron spoke. "Five. One. Seven. Three. Nine. Two. One. Seven. Nine."

"Code confirmed." An electronically distorted voice greeted him. "Hello."

Herron smiled. Though he'd never met the person on the other end of the line, it was strangely comforting to speak to his handler. "I was unsuccessful. I killed several of the targets and then I was captured. They interrogated me and injected me with an unknown agent. Three are still alive and escaped before I could free myself."

There was a pause. "I'll task other assets to finish the job. Abort your mission and remain on standby."

"I can finish—"

The receiver beeped in his ear. Herron slammed the handset back into its cradle with as much force as he could muster, exited the phone booth and returned to the car. He couldn't believe his handler would allocate other operatives to complete his mission, but orders or not, that didn't change anything.

Now he had a score to settle and a reputation to protect.

3

HERRON DIDN'T LIKE ATLANTA. It was the home of Coca Cola — a former addiction of his — and it held too many memories of an ex-girlfriend he'd rather forget. Unfortunately, it was also home to the Center for Disease Control, so it couldn't be avoided. He just hoped that the visit to this facility with Kearns was worth the trip.

"Ready?" Herron looked at Kearns, weighing up again whether he could trust her.

She nodded. "As I'll ever be."

Together they crossed the street towards the impressive-looking building and entered the lobby. There were plenty of people around, the same as any corporate lobby around lunchtime, though a significant security presence isolated the heart of the facility from the public. A checkpoint and gates requiring staff passes were the most visible deterrents.

"Fuck." Kearns stopped walking and stared at the security gate. "I don't have my staff pass. They took it from me when they kidnapped me."

Herron stared at her. He couldn't believe they'd driven five hours on the promise of a breakthrough and couldn't get inside the building. He'd have to wing it. "We'll talk our way in."

He headed towards the security desk. Kearns fell in next to him and as they approached the desk Herron tucked his left hand into his pocket. He couldn't let anyone see his mutilated thumb, although there was nothing he could do about the cuts and bruises to his face. Behind the desk sat an overweight guard with his arms crossed.

"Good afternoon." Herron smiled. "I'm in from UC Berkeley. Dr Kearns is going to give me a tour."

The guard scratched his salt-and-pepper mustache and scrutinized Herron's battered visage. "Having a bad day, sir?"

"Never get on the wrong side of a fellow professor with an outdated theory." Herron broadened his smile.

"Sure." The guard uncrossed his arms, revealing the name on his name tag – Murray. Then he looked at Kearns. "Dr Kearns, you know how to sign him in and take him through."

"Ah, yes. There's the problem." There was a note of caution in Kearns' voice, like she'd had run-ins with this guy before. "I left my pass at home."

"Again?" Murray sighed. "I'll make you out another temporary pass. But you can't take your friend through. No pass, no entry. Same rules for everyone."

Kearns threw up her hands. "But you know who I—"

"But I don't know your friend." Murray looked at Herron. "I missed your name before."

"Professor Sebastian Long." Herron didn't hesitate. "As I said, I work out in California and Erica kindly agreed to host me while I'm in town."

Murray grunted and looked down at his computer. His hands danced across the keyboard and he concentrated hard on the screen for a few moments, glancing up at Herron and then back down at the screen. Herron kept his face neutral as they waited, although Kearns was struggling to hide her confusion.

As Murray worked the computer, Herron looked around, feigning disinterest. He scanned the other people walking through the lobby. Then, his eyes settled on a commemorative plaque mounted on the wall near the elevator bay. It said something about the building being re-opened by the CDC Director, George Haskell, after refurbishment a year ago.

Herron smiled and played the averages. "Is this going to take much longer? Director Haskell didn't tell me it'd be so much effort to get inside."

Murray glanced up at him, eyes wide. Then he grunted, reached into a drawer to grab two small plastic cards and held them out. "Sorry for the misunderstanding, Professor Long. These will give you both access to the facility. I hope you won't report this misunderstanding to the Director."

"Oh, no problem at all!" Herron clapped his hands together, took the pass and then turned to face Kearns. "Erica, I think you know the way from here?"

Kearns forced a smile and took her pass. "Sure do. Thanks again for understanding and giving me a break, Murray."

The guard gave them a half-assed wave goodbye and they walked to the security barriers, swiped their cards and then went through. An elevator was just arriving and when the crowd of hungry staff had disembarked, Herron and Kearns stepped inside. Kearns pressed the button for her floor, the doors closed and they were alone.

"How do you know Seb Long?" Kearns blurted out the words as soon as the elevator doors had closed.

Herron shrugged. "His name was on one of the reports in that folder. He was also mentioned in the pre-briefing for my mission."

She scoffed. "Professor Long is one of the world's leading experts in immunovirology. He's a genius. But he's also a terrible recluse."

"I know." Herron smiled. "There are about five photos of him in existence. I knew they wouldn't be able to find any pictures of him online."

"And what about Haskell?" Kearns raised an eyebrow. "How did you know the security staff are all shit scared of him?"

"Oh, that was just luck."

Kearns shook her head in disbelief and they rode up in silence. Herron wasn't often required to talk his way into tight places to complete his missions, but he was more than capable of it. The fact that he'd been with a CDC employee had lowered Murray's guard, so all Herron had had to do was give him a bit more of a nudge. Name dropping his boss had worked and the rent-a-cop had folded.

The elevator came to a stop and the doors opened. Herron followed Kearns out and into the corridors of her workplace. It was like a mix of hospital and spaceship, a temple of high technology dedicated to keeping humanity safe from threats of accident, nature or deliberate intent. Seeing it, Herron was more confident that Kearns could help him find the next lead amidst the information he'd found and from the tests she was going to run.

They reached Kearns' office. It was large, with a desk and meeting table that could seat eight, but few personal effects. They didn't linger in the office long. He followed Kearns across the room to a door and waited as she punched a six-digit code into a keypad, her body shielding the combination from his sight. The door clicked open, and she gestured Herron into the large room beyond – a fully equipped lab.

"Undress to your underwear and sit over there." Kearns pointed at a simple plastic chair in the corner of the lab. "I'll dress your wounds and then see what I can find out."

Herron hesitated. He'd probably be able to do a

better job of tending his own wounds. He'd had more practice. "Do you know what you're doing?"

She smirked slightly, the first time he'd seen her smile. "Of course I do. You think I usually ask strangers to undress without good reason?"

Herron nodded and removed the clothes he'd stolen from the compound. Kearns located a first aid kit before setting to work spreading disinfectant gel over his smaller cuts and dressing them with sticking plaster. If he winced then, that pain was nothing compared to the agony of her cleaning the blood crusted around the bed of his thumbnail. He inhaled sharply as she applied basic adhesive bandages to the digit, then dressed the wound in his thigh.

"That's the best I can do." She tossed bloodied gauze into the trash can in the corner. "You should get checked out by a doctor."

"I'll be fine." Herron sat in a chair. "Don't waste any more time worrying about me, just figure out what we're dealing with."

Kearns nodded and started to work. She organized the papers Herron had found into neat stacks, then began to use her computer. Her hands moved fast across the keyboard as her eyes darted between the screen and the plethora of documents. Herron knew interrupting would do little good and Kearns would get to her answers faster without distraction, so he let her work.

The time and effort spent at the compound and the long drive to Atlanta had taken it out of him. He'd learned from his time in the Special Forces to get sleep whenever it was on offer, and if the fanatics' timetable for the release of their pandemic was still on track, he wouldn't get many more chances. While she worked, he made himself comfortable and closed his eyes.

Sometime later, something tapped him on the shoulder. His eyes shot open to see a hand holding a syringe. He struck like a cobra, gripping the wrist and yanking it back hard. A woman cried out in pain and as Herron shot to his feet, his mind caught up with his physical reactions. He was in Kearns' lab and he was twisting her wrist.

"What the hell?" Kearns pulled her hand away as his grip slackened. "I was just trying to wake you to take a blood sample!"

"Muscle memory." He let go entirely and blinked a few times. She was lucky she hadn't been seriously hurt. "You need to be more careful."

"Clearly." Kearns rubbed her wrist. "I deal with deadly pathogens every day and I've never been hurt in my lab until I met you."

Herron gestured for her to take the sample. "I killed the last person who tried to stick something in me."

"That's why you need a safe word." She gave a nervous laugh as she pulled back on the plunger, drawing his blood. "Now, let's see what we can find."

* * *

When next Herron opened his eyes, Kearns was calling his name from across the room. He couldn't blame her for keeping some distance, given what had happened the last time she'd woken him. He rubbed his eyes, feeling like he'd only slept for thirty seconds, but knowing he'd be much better for the rest.

"You've been busy." He glanced around the office. There was paper strewn around the bench and a whole lot of equipment had been used. "How long have I been asleep?"

"A few more hours." She stepped closer, clutching a single sheet of paper. "It's early in the evening."

"So, what's the diagnosis, Doc?"

Her expression darkened. "I've got bad news, Mitch. You've been injected with something hazardous."

"I didn't think it was rainbows and candy."

She held out the paper. "This is the blood report. I've also studied the files you captured and done some lab work of my own. They were very thorough with their record keeping, which was helpful. I need to run some more tests, but it looks like they've injected you with the same thing they're intending to spread — weaponized smallpox."

Herron frowned. "Didn't they eradicate smallpox in the 1970s or 1980s?"

"Sure, but..." Her voice trailed off. "Look, the original virus had two strains. The least serious had a five per cent mortality rate. The other was far more lethal and about a third of those who were infected died. But a vaccine was developed and both strains were eradicated. The last known case was in the 1980s"

"Go on."

"This strain they've given you has four fundamental differences from the original strains. It's more virulent, more lethal and far slower to act."

Herron raised an eyebrow. "That's only three."

"The normal smallpox vaccine is ineffective on it." Kearns' voice was grave. "I'm going to need to put you into quarantine until we figure out what to do."

"That's not going to happen, Erica." Herron shook his head. "Just tell me how they plan to spread it."

"Don't you get it? It spreads through people like you! They've turned you into a biological weapon!" She paused and took a breath. "They've timed the virus to spread from the day of their choosing. Almost nothing will happen until that point and the carriers aren't contagious, but after it activates it will spread like wildfire."

"How does that even work?"

She sighed. "It is dormant – latent. There's a whole lot of big words and phrases to explain it, but it basically lies dormant inside of your cells until it activates. Then it goes crazy. Think about it like Herpes. You can have it for life, but it might only activate a few times. There's plenty of other examples, like HIV and influenza, but this will ruin the planet."

Herron clenched his teeth as the final piece fell into place. "And they've designed it to trigger on a particular day."

She nodded. "Yes. There's plenty of references to that in their documentation and I can see it in the lab tests, but I just don't know when."

"I do." Herron stood. "World Environment Day – three days from now. Their leader told me so. On that day – their 'reckoning' – it goes full throttle and I'll start to spread it?"

"You and anyone else who's carrying it." Kearns paused. "I've no way of knowing the exact effects, but I think it'll take over your body quickly and then get to work spreading. It will tear through the population in a few days. This is the Omega Strain: lethal, easily spreadable, unstoppable. It's a doomsday weapon."

"You're sure it's synthetic?"

"Mostly."

"How many people could make it?"

Kearns thought. "Only two or three people on the planet could develop something this complex."

"You know their names?"

"Sure, but –"

"Okay." Herron moved for the door then stopped suddenly. "I'll need the code to get out."

Kearns looked at him in disbelief. "Excuse me?"

"The guy who developed this is the first step to finding Freeman. So I have to find him."

"Mitch, I need you to submit to CDC quarantine. This is a high-priority threat, I can get a lot of brilliant people working on it. We might crack it in time, but I—"

"If you crack it, it won't be in time to protect the broader population. Not without eradicating

Freeman and the other carriers." Herron shook his head. "This isn't a debate. Give me the names and give me the door code and you'll give me a greater chance of finding Freeman."

If she didn't tell him, he'd have to use other means to track down those capable of designing such a bioweapon. Assuming he could get out of the room.

Conflict played out on Kearns' face. Finally, she let out a long sigh, walked to the keypad, punched in five digits and then turned to Herron with a defiant look on her face. "One condition."

"Seriously?" Herron glared at her. He was losing patience.

"If you won't submit to quarantine, you'll need constant observation to limit the risk of outbreak. For that, you'll need a qualified doctor. You also have no idea what you're looking for. I solve both of those problems." Her eyes went unfocused for a second, as if her career was flashing before them. "If you want the last number, take me with you."

Herron smirked. "I know five out of six numbers now, that only leaves ten possibilities to try."

"And after the second failed attempt the whole building goes into lockdown." She tilted her head and raised her eyebrows, sporting a smirk of her own. "Take. Me. With. You."

Herron clenched his jaw. Like it or not, he was out of his depth here. He needed a guide to this world of scientific formulas and synthetic viruses. "Fine. Now give me the names and open the door."

"Professor Fabian Bouchard would be my first

guess." Her face clouded with emotion. "He works for the CDC and he's been on extended leave lately. I also recognize his work – the documents you gave me have his fingerprints all over them."

"You know him?" She nodded. "Okay. Time to pay him a visit."

"He lives close to me." Kearns punched the final code button.

That's when the alarms started.

* * *

Herron looked at Kearns. "You said we had two wrong attempts."

"It was the right code." She pushed the door and it swung open. "I think they might have figured out you're not Sebastian Long."

"That took them... a long time. Let's get out of here. I don't want to have to deal with an army of security."

They made for the elevator bank they'd arrived in, the alarm blaring every few seconds. Several of Kearns' colleagues were also working late, it seemed, because a few people poked their head out of a lab or office. No one else was attempting to leave. Once they reached the elevator, Kearns pressed the call button.

Herron saw her hand was shaking. "This is probably your last chance to walk away. Go back to your lab."

She seemed tempted by his offer for a second, then clenched her fists and stood a little taller. "Not a chance, I—"

The elevator pinged and Herron looked to the doors as they opened. The car was full of four armed security personal sporting grim expressions. They spilled out and cast a hard eye at Herron and Kearns. Though he might be able to take a few of them down, he didn't like his chances against all four of them.

"The building is in lockdown." One of the guards scowled at them. "Back to your office!"

Herron smiled and nodded at the guard as they pushed on down the corridor, headed for Kearns' office. Herron didn't waste a second. He raced to the stairwell entrance, opened the door and started taking the stairs down two at a time. Kearns was on his heels, breathing heavily. She didn't seem overly fit, despite her lean frame. Herron tried to slow down for the rest of the way.

"Where are we going?" Kearns' voice had an edge of stress and fear. "They said the whole building was in lockdown."

"Parking garage. I've never seen a boom gate I can't drive through."

They reached the basement and jogged down the corridor, following the signs to the carpark. Then, just ahead of them, two security guards rounded the corner. The first was an athletic-looking man who looked like he could handle himself. The second was Murray, the guard who'd signed them into the building.

"Dr Kearns, Professor Long." Murray raised a hand in greeting. "Can we talk with you for just a second?"

"Of course, but we'll need to be quick." Kearns halted and looked at Herron. "I was just getting Professor Long on his way. We got talking and lost track of time."

"That must have been some conversation." The other guard stepped edged closer to them. His nametag identified him as Lavery. "There's a matter we need to clear up."

Murray nodded. "Thing is, we just spoke to someone at UC Berkeley Campus. He was calling to talk to someone up on nine. Said his name was Professor Long..."

Murray's hand drifted down to his weapon and Herron tensed. He didn't want to have to kill these men. They were just doing their job. But he didn't have time to mess around either. Herron stepped forward and, at the same time, Lavery raised his hand and palm outward in a 'stop' gesture. That was his mistake.

Herron gripped Lavery's wrist with his left hand and pulled on it. The guard stumbled forward and Herron delivered a right jab to the man's stomach. Lavery grunted as the wind was driven out of him, but Herron gave him no time to recover. He placed his foot behind the guard's ankle and gave him a firm shove. Lavery fell and his head struck the floor.

Herron locked eyes with Murray, who'd taken a step back and was struggling to unbutton his holster and draw his weapon. Herron had banked on exactly that. He knew security personnel practiced so infrequently with their weapons that, under stress, a holster retention button might as well be the Gordian knot.

Herron had no such trouble. He crouched down, unholstered Lavery's weapon and leveled it at Murray. "Calm down."

"Hey, buddy, I don't want trouble." Murray dropped his hands to his side. "We're just doing our job, you know?"

Herron kept his pistol trained on Murray as he held out a hand. "Give me your weapon. Move slowly."

"There's no way you'll get out of this facility." Murray finally managed to unholster his weapon and handed it over. "The police are on their way."

Herron stuffed the spare pistol into his belt. "Cuff yourself to your partner and shut up if you want to walk away from this."

Murray looked like he might resist, but after a second he reached down to his belt and drew a pair of handcuffs from their pouch. He tethered his wrist to that of his partner, who was still stunned on the floor. Herron stepped closer and took possession of Lavery's cuffs. They'd come in handy, he was sure. The last thing he did was toss their radios down the hall.

"Go." Herron gestured for Kearns to move in the direction of the carpark, while he backed away from the guards slowly and never took his pistol of them. They didn't move.

Herron backed away after her. Kearns pushed through a door at the end of the passage and Herron followed into the parking garage. As soon as the door swung closed he broke into a run, looking for any vehicle he knew could be easily hot-wired. Unfortunately, it seemed the scientists at the CDC mostly drove expensive Japanese and European cars, which were much harder to steal.

"Uh, Mitch?" Kearns spoke from behind him.

"What?"

"I was on my lunch break when they kidnapped me." She pointed at a new model Audi.

He squinted at her. "That's yours?"

She nodded. "And I keep a spare key taped to the back of one of the rims."

Herron smiled. "I'm driving."

4

HERRON SMILED as he finally cast eyes on Lyndon Pratt, an arms dealer who'd grown too big and resisted all Government attempts to make him retire or relocate quietly. The arms dealer had supplied heavy artillery to most of the street gangs and the drug runners on the Eastern Seaboard, making life hell for the authorities. But now Herron had him in the sights of his silenced SMG.

After a slow breath, Herron squeezed the trigger. A burst of fire ripped into Pratt's head, causing him to stumble...but he kept his feet. Herron's target turned and looked in his direction. How could he take a full burst to the head and remain standing? Herron fired another burst, then another. Each round tore bloody chunks of flesh from Pratt's face, but somehow the gun runner stayed upright.

Herron snarled and unloaded the full magazine

into him. The SMG kicked into his shoulder and shots sprayed all over Pratt's upper torso, but still they didn't stop him. The SMG ran dry. Herron tossed it to the ground and drew his pistol. That, too, was fired until empty and to no better effect. Pratt closed to within ten yards and Herron unsheathed his combat knife with a guttural scream...

The scream continued as Herron opened his eyes. The digital alarm clock on the bedside table bled pale yellow light into the otherwise dark motel room. It was 2:03 AM. He lay there for another few moments, thankful his nightmares were over for another night. He'd always assumed they were part of the business, although working alone meant there was no one he could ask.

It hadn't taken long for him and Kearns to arrive at Fabian Bouchard's house in Alpharetta – a leafy and quiet neighborhood north of Atlanta – but when they'd driven past they'd discovered Bouchard was throwing a party. Herron couldn't just walk in with so many potential witnesses, so he'd had to leave him alone for the night. Herron had turned the car around, found a motel and paid cash for two rooms.

With a sigh, Herron climbed out of bed and walked to the small bathroom. He showered, gasping as the water stung his wounds, but his mind was elsewhere. He had bigger things to worry about, like a weapon of mass destruction ticking away inside him and a lot of people he needed to kill in very little time.

He dressed in his clothes from the previous day and pocketed the wad of cash he'd found at the compound, then stuffed the better of the two pistols he'd taken from the CDC security guards down the back of his jeans, covering it with the t-shirt and jacket. The other weapon he stashed in the backpack that contained the folder full of files.

Herron left the room, paused briefly to check nothing was amiss and then moved to Kearns' room. He knocked on her door, loudly enough that she'd wake up but not so loud as to rouse anyone else in the motel. At check in, the receptionist had asked if they wanted a room together. Kearns had laughed and Herron had shaken his head. If only she knew the truth.

Eventually, Kearns answered the door, wrapped in a complementary motel robe. Her brown hair was a tousled mess and she looked unimpressed. "It's the middle of the night."

He couldn't have cared less. He pushed into the room and closed the door behind him. "We're leaving in fifteen minutes. Go have a shower."

She crossed her arms over her chest and stared at him. "Mitch, do you know what time it is?"

"It's 2:16 AM. Now we're leaving in fourteen minutes."

"I'll need more time than that. I need to wash my hair. And we should at least get something to eat..." Her voice died when she saw the look on his face.

He waited impassively as she huffed, turned and

walked to the bathroom. After the door had slammed and the shower was running, he collapsed onto the two-seater sofa. It was the only feature of the room except for the bed, a coffee table, and a TV. He assessed the food situation – a mix of junk Kearns had scattered on the coffee table – and chose a chocolate bar.

As he munched on the candy, he reached for the TV remote and turned on the news. An ambulance had driven off the side of a mountain, some politician or other had been exposed as corrupt... nothing very interesting. Herron grew bored, opened the backpack and started to flick through the files. He hadn't finished searching them earlier and, though most were scientific gibberish, some provided useful information about the fanatics.

He was taken aback when he read one of the last sheets of paper in the folder. His eyes widened and he looked at it for a long time, not quite believing what he was seeing. A broad smile broke out across his face, until he overheard the next story on the news and his smile turned into a grimace. The cutaway box in the top of the screen showed the CDC headquarters in Atlanta as the anchor looked earnestly into the camera and read from his autocue.

"Police are still no closer to identifying the armed man who took a senior scientist hostage and evaded arrest at the Center for Disease Control headquarters in Atlanta. He was last seen driving an Audi A7, license plate DAE252. Anyone with information should contact police, who stress that the man is armed and is not to be approached."

"Fuck." Herron turned off the TV and tossed the remote on the table. He sat with his eyes closed and rubbed his temples with his forefingers. He couldn't get a break.

"What?" Kearns called out from the bathroom. The door was now open and the shower had stopped.

"Seems I'm a fugitive and you're my prisoner." He opened his eyes again and stood. "They've identified your car, so I'll have to find us another. I'll meet you out front."

"Well, you're the second worst jailer I've had in the last few days." Kearns' voice dripped with sarcasm.

Herron folded the piece of paper and put it in his pocket. Then he picked up his backpack, opened the door and stepped outside. He scanned the car park, searching for a suitable vehicle and anyone who'd get in the way of him taking it. The motel was small and less than half full, so Herron's options were limited. He settled on an old Hyundai. It was a downgrade from Kearns' Audi, but he needed something he could lift easily.

Herron dug in the backpack for his bump keys, crossed the car park and crouched down next to the driver's door. The low-quality lock on the old Hyundai surrendered in less than thirty seconds. He opened the door, tossed the backpack into the rear seat and climbed inside. The bump keys started the vehicle as easily as they had opened it.

Only moments after the car was running there was a knock on the passenger-side window. Herron leaned over to unlock the door. Kearns opened it and climbed inside. Herron could instantly smell the scent of the hotel shampoo, some flower or another. It took slightly longer to realize that she was radiating fury.

"What's wrong?"

"You ate the Snickers." Her voice was full of indignation. "I was saving that."

* * *

Herron parked across the street and a half-dozen houses down from Bouchard's place. Normally he'd have felt exposed, given the street was full of expensive cars that made the old Hyundai look out of place. But it was almost 3.00 AM, the time most people were at the low point of individual readiness, and the street was quiet. Herron would be done long before the neighbors stirred.

They watched the house for a quarter hour, to make sure there was nothing amiss. Usually, Herron would stake out a target for days, but he didn't have time. It probably wouldn't matter, because except for dim light bleeding from one room the house seemed dark and peaceful. He was probably passed out drunk after the party.

"Wait here." Herron glanced at Kearns. "This shouldn't take long."

He unbuckled his seatbelt and got out of the vehicle. After checking his pistol was still in place down the back of his jeans, Herron crossed the street. Bouchard's place was the best house on the street, suggesting he had done well out of the disease business or that he had another earner on the side...

Herron walked down the side of the house, hoping the crunching of his footfalls on the gravel path wouldn't wake anyone. He unlatched the side gate and let himself into the backyard. It was a mess. The wooden deck was littered with empty wine bottles and plates of half-eaten food that were attracting bugs.

By the looks of it, Bouchard's party had been a blast, but it would pale next to the experience Herron had in store for him. Herron tried the sliding glass door and smiled when he found it unlocked. Waiting for the end of the party had cost him a few precious hours, but it meant the drunk homeowner had left himself more vulnerable to predators.

Herron entered the house with his pistol raised and moved through the open-plan living area. Though he expected to find Bouchard in bed, there was no telling who else might be in the house. He rounded the corner into the kitchen, which was where the light had been coming from. The stove was on, though nothing sat atop the burner flame. Herron became more alert.

"Get out of my house!" A man leaped out of the walk-in pantry. He wore nothing but his underwear and was holding a pot, which he tossed at Herron.

Hot liquid splashed over Herron, giving Bouchard

the chance to run past him. Herron gritted his teeth against the spike of pain. The soup that had splashed over him was hot, not scalding, and nowhere near as dangerous as if the scientist escaped from the house. Bouchard was screaming and risked rousing the neighbors. He cursed and chased after the scientist.

He gained on the Bouchard with each step, but his target still almost made it to the door before Herron crash-tackled him. He landed hard on top of Bouchard, losing his grip on the pistol as they sprawled to the ground. Bouchard struggled, throwing weak punches and thrashing his body to dislodge Herron, but none of it did any good. Herron needed to end this.

He fended off the scientist's blows with his left hand and reached down to grip Bouchard's arm with his right. Using his knee as leverage, he positioned the other man's arm just so, then hissed loudly, "If you don't stop fighting I'm going to break your arm."

Bouchard ignored him and kept struggling. With no further warning, Herron pulled back on Bouchard's arm and the force of his knee pressing into it broke his ulna with a sickening crack. Bouchard howled and used his intact arm to cradle his broken one. As the scientist dealt with his new problem, Herron stumbled off him, found his pistol and aimed it at Bouchard.

Herron climbed to his feet, gun leveled at Bouchard. "Let's try this again. If you move an inch, I'll shoot you."

"You broke my arm!" Bouchard's voice was full of panic and accusation. "You broke my fucking arm!"

"I told you to stop resisting." Herron was tired of this man. "If you try anything else, things will get worse."

All fight disappeared from Bouchard and he sagged. "Take whatever you want, please, just don't hurt me."

Herron sighed. If only all this were as simple as a robbery. Keeping Bouchard covered with one hand, he searched through his pocket with the other, removing the handcuffs he'd taken from Murray the security guard. He tossed them on the floor next to Bouchard. The scientist looked down at them but remained still. Herron looked around for something to cuff Bouchard to and settled on the decorative metalwork of the dining table.

Herron spoke slowly, aware that Bouchard might be in shock and struggling to understand instruction. "Cuff your left hand to the inside frame of your dining table."

Bouchard followed the instructions, cursing and crying out in pain the whole time. He fumbled with the cuffs, moaning in pain, but eventually succeeded in tethering his broken arm to the table. Herron was satisfied he was secure – any movement would lead to torturous pain and any attempt to escape would force Bouchard to drag the whole table with him.

"Is there anyone else in the house?" Herron took a step closer to Bouchard and pressed the pistol against his temple. "If you lie to me, they die."

"No." Bouchard sobbed loudly. "Please, don't hurt me. Why are you here? What do you want from me?"

Herron ignored the questions and looked down at his stained t-shirt. "Who eats soup at this time of night?"

* * *

"Get him to confirm what we're dealing with." Herron spoke quietly to Kearns, whom he'd fetched from the car. "We need to know who he gave it to."

"Can I put his arm in a sling first?" Kearns regarded Bouchard with the pity she might reserve for a stray dog. "It'll only take me a moment."

Herron was inclined to deny her request, but didn't want an argument. And there was some logic in her request. Bouchard was now seated at the dining table without cuffs, on the understanding that if he moved an inch his other arm would be broken too. That knowledge, combined with a sling, would make him less likely to act out.

"Fine." He nodded at Kearns and crossed his arms. "But don't take too long."

Kearns rigged a sling out of a kitchen towel and a splint out of two wooden spoons. Bouchard was thankful, though he did cry out in pain, earning a glare of warning from Herron. It was time to get to down to business. He'd searched the rest of the house before bringing Kearns in from the car and now he didn't want to be here any longer than necessary.

Herron picked up the folder full of files, walked over to the dining table and slammed them down. "I've been injected with a highly virulent smallpox strain that's resistant to the vaccine. It will take over my body and make me a carrier in three days."

Bouchard stared at him, open-mouthed, then broke into nervous laughter. "You're joking. We wiped out smallpox decades ago."

"You know, I once went to a zoo in Texas." Herron switched his tone to light, chatty. "It only had one animal, a little dog."

Bouchard's face was a picture of confusion. "What?"

"It was a shit zoo." Herron's face changed, dark with menace. He leaned in close, voice barely a whisper. "That was me joking. Just so you know the difference."

Bouchard closed his eyes and shook his head. "I know nothing about—"

Herron pulled the pistol out and put it on the table. "That same virus inside me is being carried by several other men, who're aiming to unleash it in less than three days. The document trail tells me that much. What I want to know from you is your role in designing the virus and who you gave it to."

"I'll talk." Bouchard sagged. "But only to her."

"All right. But you try anything..." Herron picked up the pistol.

Kearns moved to the table and the two scientists began rustling through the papers. Herron took little interest in their chatter as they flicked through the papers, but he did watch them closely. After a few minutes, Bouchard's face turned pale – Herron would even go as far as to say terrified.

"What is it?" Herron broke up their conversation.

"I... This isn't my design." Bouchard sounded like a grieving man struggling to come to terms with his loss. "It's been modified."

"How?" Kearns' voice had an insistence in it that Herron hadn't heard before.

"I designed weaponized smallpox that's resistant to the vaccine, but otherwise like other strands." Bouchard was clearly afraid. "But that was like finger-painting. This is the Mona Lisa."

Fear twisted in the pit of Herron's stomach. If the man who'd brought the threat of smallpox back to the world was this scared by the Omega Strain, then it was an even more terrifying proposition than he'd first thought. "Can it be stopped?"

"No. I told you, my design rendered the vaccine useless." Bouchard shook his head. "This strain is even more dangerous. Someone vastly more talented than me has modified it. It will stay latent, but if it reaches maturity in the hosts' bodies it will spread and devastate the general population. It will be more lethal than any outbreak in human history."

"Who'd you sell the virus to?"

"It's not that simple." Bouchard seemed to sense the conversation was getting to its pointy end. "Science is a shared endeavor and I can't claim to—"

Herron raised the pistol and aimed it at

Bouchard's head. "I'm losing patience. Who'd you sell the virus to?"

Bouchard nodded frantically. "His name was Kyle Glennon. He belongs to a group that claimed they were environmentalists. That's all I know."

Herron paused, then smiled like a hyena and dug into his pocket. He pulled out the sheet of paper he'd pocketed at the motel, which he'd removed from Freeman's folder. The sheet had a list of names and Glennon's name was on it. He was sure the name of every fanatic was. But, without being able to match the names to a physical description, he couldn't figure out which of them he'd already killed at the compound or narrow down the search to find them.

Herron held out the cell phone he'd confiscated from Bouchard. "Call Glennon. Tell him you need to meet at noon, at the usual place, wherever that is. If you try to warn him, you die."

Bouchard took the phone, dialed and put it to his ear. Herron snatched it away, switched it to speaker and placed it on the table. He wanted to hear every word and be ready to intervene if Bouchard tried anything. The phone rang for a long time and Herron was just starting to doubt it would be answered when someone picked up.

For a second there was only breathing, then a man spoke. "What do you want? I was sleeping, Fabian. Our business is done."

Bouchard hesitated. "There's a problem. We need to meet."

"Our business is done." Glennon's tone suggested his position was final.

"If you want to use my... product... in a few days then you'll meet with me and listen to what I have to say." Bouchard paused. "It's a matter of life and death."

On the other end of the line, Glennon sighed. "If you're wasting my time, it'll be on your head. I paid you to deliver a product and then forget I ever existed. 11:00 AM at the usual place."

The line went dead and Herron lowered the pistol. Bouchard sagged with relief and started to cry. Fabian Bouchard was a smart man, not a hard one. He wasn't trained or conditioned to withstand this sort of treatment. He'd done something foolish and probably made a lot of money, but it had cost him everything.

"Write down the address of the meeting point for me." Herron barked at Bouchard and then turned to Kearns. "Pack up. We're leaving. We'll meet you in the car."

"Okay." Relief swept over her face as she swallowed his lie. She quickly gathered up the paperwork and left.

Herron waited until Kearns had departed, then spoke again. "I want you to write down the address of the normal meeting place."

Bouchard scribbled it down and Herron scooped up the paper. He walked behind the broken scientist, heading for the door. "Goodbye, Professor."

Bouchard nodded without looking round. If he

had turned, he would've seen the pistol pointed at the back of his head. "I'm very sorry."

Herron pulled the trigger and Bouchard slumped forward in his chair. He paused only long enough to say one word. "143."

5

HERRON CLIMBED INSIDE THE HYUNDAI, buckled his seatbelt and looked over at Kearns. She was clutching the folder of files like a life raft and tears streaked down her face as she stared out the windshield. He didn't have time for hysterics. If she'd heard the gunshot, every neighbor within a block would've too, and the police would be on their way.

With a shrug, Herron started the car and pulled away. He drove at the speed limit and got them on to the highway. He was excited by the prospect of finding the next link in the chain, so he dug into his pocket for the cell phone he'd taken from Bouchard and the piece of paper with the address of the meeting point.

He held them both out to Kearns using the same hand. "I need directions. Can you pull up a map?"

He glanced at her a few times, but Kearns made no move to take the phone and just kept staring straight ahead. Herron sighed. He'd lied to her at the house to keep things moving, but surely she'd known Bouchard's fate was sealed when he admitted his role in designing the virus? He gave up, held down the button on the phone and told the virtual assistant to pull up the address.

They drove on in silence. He was pleased to have his first firm link back to the fanatics since he'd screwed up at the compound. If he could crack Glennon he might be able to deal with Freeman and his followers before the Omega Strain could be unleashed. Right now, though, they had time to kill, and they had to eat at some point...

He pulled into the first diner he saw, parked and looked over at Kearns. "I need you to pull yourself together."

"He gave you what you wanted." Kearns' voice was laced with pure disdain. "You didn't have to kill him."

"He helped to develop the virus. He had to die."

Kearns recoiled like she'd been slapped. "You can't just go around killing everyone who's involved in this! It's evil!"

"I never said I wasn't evil." Herron shrugged. "I'm going to wipe out Freeman and everyone else who is on that list. They're all linked to this. It's that simple."

"Men like you—"

"Men like me get our hands dirty so you don't have to." Herron lost his patience and snapped. "Men like me keep people like you safe."

"It's wrong. There has to be a less bloody solution."

"Do you think I care about your opinion?" He stared at her. "This virus could wipe out millions and it's my job to stop it. Now, do you want to eat something or not?"

Herron kept his face impassive as Kearns stared back at him hard, then nodded. They exited the car, walked into the diner and Herron led them to the booth furthest from the door. He sat with his back to the wall, which gave him the best view of the door and his surroundings. It was an old habit that'd served him well over the years.

A waitress arrived at their table 20 seconds after they'd sat down. "You guys after some food? Or just coffee?"

"Both, please. Coffee, eggs, tomato, bacon and toast..." Herron glanced at Kearns. She nodded coldly. He looked back at the waitress and smiled. "For both of us. Thanks."

"No problem." She scribbled their order on her notepad, seemingly accustomed to feuding couples stopping by for breakfast. "It shouldn't take long."

Herron kept his smile until the waitress departed, then settled into silence. Kearns could give him the cold shoulder if she liked. She'd either deal with his way of working or she wouldn't, but he didn't see any sense in wasting time on it. He simply stared out the window and made a mental checklist of all the other things he did have to worry about.

Soon after their coffee arrived, one of those things

rolled into the diner's parking lot. A Georgia State Police cruiser pulled in and parked next to the old Hyundai. Herron drained his coffee, his eyes locked onto the cruiser and the two cops who climbed out of it. Their gaze settled on his Hyundai for a second and then they headed for the diner.

"What is it?" Kearns had tension in her voice.

"Two cops just parked next to our car and paid it too much attention for my liking." Herron put his cup down as the diner door opened, the chime sounded and the cops walked in. They wandered over to the waitress and made a show of talking casually to her. "Wait here. If they come over, don't say or do anything."

Herron slid along the booth seat and stood. He needed to test if the cops were here for more than coffee, he so headed in the direction of the bathroom. He could sense the eyes of the cops boring into him. He wanted to provoke a reaction from them. If they pursued him or cornered Kearns, he'd have to act. If they didn't, he and Kearns could eat their meal in peace.

Once inside the bathroom, he unzipped his jeans and used the urinal. A few seconds later, the larger of the two cops entered. Herron glanced at him. "Morning."

"Morning to you." The cop whistled as he stood at the urinal next to him and unzipped. "How're you today?"

Herron looked straight ahead at the white wall tiles. He still wasn't sure if the cops had a particular interest in him, or just a passing one. He'd find out. He finished, flushed and walked to the washbasin. He was halfway through washing his hands when the cop appeared alongside him. He had only stood at the urinal for a moment, barely long enough to use it.

"All yours." Herron gestured at the basin, smiled at the officer and headed for the exit. He was reaching for the door handle when the cop placed a hand on his shoulder.

"Just hold up a second, sir." The cop removed his hand. "I wanted to ask you a few questions, away from the lady out there."

Herron sighed and turned. The policeman had one hand on his holster. There was a lot of ways he could play this, but only one that wouldn't deprive him of the time he needed to stop Freeman and his people. He made his decision.

"You should wash your hands." Herron lashed an elbow at the cop's head and the lawman was out before he hit the ground. "Sorry."

Herron cuffed him to a drainpipe and headed back to the booth, where two things had happened: their food had arrived and the second officer had started talking to Kearns. He was a smaller man than his partner and to the untrained eye he'd look relaxed, but Herron knew better. The moment he'd seen Herron emerge from the bathroom ahead of his partner, the cop had tensed for action.

"I think your partner ate a bad burrito." Herron smiled at the cop and then turned to Kearns, wondering if she was still pissed enough at him to have spoken to the cop. "Ready?"

The cop placed a hand on his holster and locked eyes with Herron. "You haven't eaten your food, sir."

"Not hungry." Herron shrugged. "I—"

The crackle of the officer's radio receiver interrupted him. *"All units, update on blue Hyundai, license plate FBA744. Occupants now believed to be connected to a homicide."*

Herron shoved the cop square in the chest – knocking him to the floor – then planted a kick in his midriff. The cop cried out in pain and curled up as Herron grabbed Kearns' hand and pulled her out of the booth. Then they were running, past the squealing waitress and gaping customers, headed for the car park.

They raced to the Hyundai and as he popped open the doors Herron caught sight of Kearns' face, pale with shock. He smiled at her thinly. "Buckle up. Things are about to get wild."

* * *

The Hyundai's rear window shattered as the cop fired several shots into it. Kearns squealed and Herron flinched, but he didn't stop. He fishtailed the vehicle out of the carpark and onto the road. The Hyundai moved as slow as a glacier, struggling up to its top speed, but gradually putting distance between them and the shooter.

Herron glanced at Kearns. "Check you're not hit."

"I'm not."

"Do it."

She scowled and started to pat herself down.

One hand on the wheel, Herron reached for his pistol. Though he was prepared for a shootout, evasion was his preference. He didn't want to kill innocent people who were just doing their job, but he wouldn't let himself be arrested either. He pulled onto the highway and floored the accelerator. The engine screamed and the Hyundai handled like a mule.

"What now, Einstein?" Kearns' voice was sharp. "I told you killing Bouchard was a mistake. Now they're onto us."

"They were onto us before that." Herron flicked his eyes to the rear-view mirror. "I appreciate you not selling me out."

"Maybe I should have. You'd be on your way back to quarantine now."

"And Freeman would be all clear to wipe out a fair slice of humanity."

"I..." Kearns thought better of talking, closed her mouth and stared ahead.

Three police cruisers had appeared behind them and were gaining fast, their engines far more powerful than the one in the Hyundai. The flashing of their light bars and the noise of their sirens drew ever closer. In a decent car, he'd outrun them, but no amount of fancy driving in the shit heap Hyundai would see them off. Herron needed another a plan.

Gripping the pistol in one hand and the wheel in the other, he looked over to Kearns. "I need you to climb over me and take the wheel."

"What?" Kearns' eyes went wide.

"I can't lose them." Herron unbuckled his seatbelt. "If you want to stop the bloodshed, this is how."

Kearns hesitated for an instant, then nodded and unbuckled her seatbelt. Herron steadied the wheel until she was crouched on her seat and then he nodded at her, removed his foot from the gas and pushed himself clear. As quickly as he could, he wriggled into the back of the car while Kearns filled the space he'd vacated.

The changeover had taken only four seconds, but the car had slowed and the cops were now close enough that Herron could see the determination in the eyes of the officer driving the nearest vehicle – the short guy from the diner. The look changed to fear as Herron knelt in the back seat and aimed his pistol through the shattered rear window.

Herron's first shot took out the front left tire, his second shredded the front right and his third went through the windshield. He'd aimed at the empty passenger seat, but the shot caused the driver to flinch, jerking the wheel enough to take the car off its line. A split-second later, the vehicle rammed into the metal side rail that rimmed the highway, out of the game.

The cops in the remaining two cars had drawn their weapons and Herron had to deal with them before they could return fire, preferably without killing them. He fired at the wheels of the next car, trying to repeat the trick. Two shots; both missed. Herron gritted his teeth. He was going to run out of rounds before he could neutralize the remaining police cruisers.

"Duck!" He dropped flat as the first of the return shots bit into the Hyundai. "You okay?"

"I'm not dead!" Kearns' voice was filled with panic.

He had to end this. Peering over the back seat, he saw one of the cop cars was still on his tail, but the other had changed lane and was using its superior acceleration to push up closer. The only thing stopping it from drawing alongside was a Ford pickup running parallel to the Hyundai, blocking its path. In the cruiser's passenger seat, a cop was waving frantically at the driver ahead to pull out of the way.

"They'll try to sideswipe you." Herron was starting to get worried. If the cop car nudged Kearns, he wasn't sure she had the skill behind the wheel to deal with it. "Keep calm."

"I am calm!"

Herron didn't argue. Instead, he popped up and fired several rounds out of the left-side window. His shots hit the tires of the Ford, blowing one out. Its driver fought the wheel as he lost control, braking and swerving, but Herron had already shifted his aim to the right-hand window. He fired again, taking out the tires of a Toyota in the next lane over. Suddenly, the police cruiser that was speeding to flank them was faced with two rapidly slowing cars and nowhere to go.

"Yes!" Kearns shouted as the cop car slammed into the rear of the Ford.

Herron checked his load. "I'm out! The bag with the other pistol is in the trunk!"

Herron eased his head up over the back seat again. The third and final cop car was glued to their tail, but this one had only one officer inside. Herron had used most of his tricks, but one last one was forming in his mind. It was risky, but he was out of options. He used the pistol to clear away the broken glass left in the back window and then eased himself through it.

"What the hell are you doing?" Kearns yelled.

"Just drive straight, and when I tell you, tap the brakes." Herron made it halfway out of the car now and ready to rock. "Now!"

Herron had hoped for a soft tap on the brakes to bring the two vehicles together. Instead he got what he'd feared. Kearns slammed them hard and Herron slid out the back of the Hyundai as the police cruiser smashed into, crunching steel and shattering glass. Herron grunted, landing hard on the hood of the police cruiser and sliding up it.

The world spun like a tumble dryer as Herron rolled over the windshield and onto the roof. He needed both hands to grab something — anything — to stop himself from falling onto the road, so he released the pistol and it bounced away behind the cars. As the two vehicles separated again, Herron gripped the flashing light bar on the roof and used it to right himself.

The cop swerved, trying to dislodge him, cutting back and forth sharply. Herron held on and slid on the roof, fighting the momentum shifts of the car. When he could, he cautiously crawled forward, aimed his right boot at the shattered windshield and kicked. The cop stopped redoubled his effort to dislodged Herron, but the glass gave way on the third try.

Herron maneuvered into the passenger seat and pulled the handbrake. The car lurched and started to lose speed as the cop lashed out with a fist. Herron blocked it, and delivered his own blow to the man's head, dazing him. As the officer lost his grip on the wheel. Herron seized control of the car and took the cop's pistol from its holster.

Herron aimed at the cop as the vehicle slowed to a stop. A hundred yards ahead, Kearns had brought the Hyundai to a halt. "If you move before I'm a speck in the distance, you die."

Herron kept the pistol trained on the cop as he stole his cuffs, pulled out the car keys and tossed them out the window. Then he took possession of the cop's cell phone and portable radio. Finally, he tore the handset from the car's fixed radio. The cop was smart. He didn't say a word or move an inch. When he was done, Herron exited the car and ran to the Hyundai.

He climbed inside and slammed the door. "Told you things were going to get a little wild."

"A little wild?" Kearns put her foot to the floor. "We could be dead!"

Herron shrugged and gave a tiny smile. "Mostly because of your driving."

* * *

"We've still got time to spare." Herron smiled at Kearns as she pulled the car to a stop, about a block away from where they were scheduled to meet Glennon.

"Want me to stay here?" There was some warmth in her voice, whereas an hour ago she'd had nothing but venom and vitriol for him.

"No. Take the bag and walk five blocks that way." Herron pointed. "I'll pick you up there when I'm done. "This won't take long."

"Okay. I'll meet you down there." She hesitated. "Thanks for not killing those cops back there, too."

"Sure." Herron shrugged. He held up the cop's pistol, ejected the clip and then slammed it home again. He pulled back the slide and chambered a round. "They didn't deserve it."

Herron exited the vehicle, stuffed the pistol down the back of his jeans and walked at a brisk pace to the meeting location. Every ache and pain from the last few days throbbed through him. Though he only had a couple of days left to live, Herron wasn't sure he'd make it that far if things continued as they were. He was used to planning a job in immaculate detail and then executing it flawlessly. The freewheeling approach of the past few days had hurt.

Bouchard had chosen an old industrial area for the meet and the streets were deserted. Most of the properties were abandoned and rusting, with fences collapsing in disrepair and weeds growing freely. Herron was glad for the isolation. He was confident he wouldn't be disturbed, but after the run-in with the cops he wasn't taking anything for granted. He wouldn't relax until he had the names he wanted from Glennon.

After a quick look to make sure he was alone, Herron leaned against a lamppost and crossed his arms, waiting. His nerves were bothering him more than usual, partly because of the police attention but mainly because of his total reliance on Glennon. Failure to squeeze the information out of him would effectively end Herron's mission and his life.

Glennon came right on time and Herron smiled when he spotted the car he was driving. It was a newer model Mercedes. He'd planned to swipe Glennon *and* the car, but hadn't expected such a nice one. The beat-up Hyundai was too damaged and hot to take any further, so this slice of luck was too good to pass up.

Herron pushed himself off the lamppost as the Mercedes stopped. He raised his left hand in greeting and kept his right by his side. Glennon kept the engine running as he opened the door and climbed out. He wore jeans, a t-shirt and a very nasty looking scowl. He was obviously angry at encountering a stranger instead of his expected contact.

"Mr Glennon!" Herron smiled broadly to counter Glennon's anger.

"Who the fuck are you, pal? Where's Bouchard?"

Herron gave a small chuckle. "Fabian is indisposed. You can deal with me instead."

Glennon's eyes widened as he realized the danger he was in. He moved twice as fast as Herron would've expected, but about half as fast as he needed to. Before Glennon could even reach his piece, Herron had drawn his pistol and was aiming it at him. Glennon froze, his eyes darting back to his car and clearly weighing up whether he should surrender, fight or flee.

Herron smiled. "Only one choice ends without a bullet inside of you."

"Look, pal. I don't want trouble." Glennon didn't choose right away. "What do you want?"

"Your car." Herron moved closer, reached into his pocket and pulled out the cuffs.

"Take it." Glennon shrugged, his gaze fixed the cuffs. "What're those for?"

"Insurance." Herron did a spinning gesture with his finger. "Turn around, put your hands behind your back and keep your eyes forward. Any movement, you die. Any resistance, you die. Okay?"

"Whatever you want." Glennon was compliant now, apparently concerned with nothing but survival. "What'd you do to Fabian?"

Herron used one hand to keep the pistol trained

on Glennon and the other to cuff him. Only then did he speak. "He told me about the virus he sold to you and your fellow crazies."

Glennon tensed. "You don't know anything. Just take the car and stay out of this or you'll live to regret it."

"I don't have many days of regrets left." Herron snarled. "I'll be in the ground with Bouchard within a few days, but I'm going to wipe you pricks out first."

"You're the guy that shot up the compound?" Glennon's voice dripped with fear and anxiety as the realization set in.

"The guy who got injected with the stuff Bouchard sold you." Herron pressed the barrel of the pistol against the back of Glennon's head.

"Well, we improved it prior to injecting ourselves with it." Glennon tensed. "But if you found Bouchard, you already know that."

"I sure do." Herron smiled. "And you're going to tell me exactly who's carrying it and what they look like."

"I'm not going to tell you shit."

Herron pistol whipped Glennon, who fell hard, unable to brace himself with his hands cuffed behind his back. It was fun to pound on the man who'd delivered the virus to the fanatics, but he needed him alive. Only Glennon could give him the physical descriptions of the names on the list. It'd help him strike out those he'd already killed and narrow down the search for those who were still alive from the dozens of men with the same names across America.

Herron spat on Glennon, walked to the Mercedes and opened the trunk. "Stand and get in the trunk. Or I keep kicking you."

Glennon mumbled something resembling acceptance and struggled to his feet. Perhaps he hoped that by being passive and compliant he might live. He couldn't be more wrong. His cooperation might achieve less pain on the way through, but the result was inevitable. Glennon climbed inside the trunk and curled into a ball.

Herron took the pistol from Glennon's waistband and slammed the trunk. With his prey in the bag, he inspected the weapon then tossed it into a drain. It was useless, a relic carried to look tough. The Mercedes was another proposition entirely, a finely designed and engineered machine he was very much looking forward to driving. He climbed inside.

It was time to talk.

6

HERRON SMILED as he gave the Mercedes one last burst of acceleration, enjoying its performance as he powered hard out of a turn and onto a quiet street. He turned to Kearns. "Are we close?"

"It's up on the left." Kearns pointed at a warehouse ahead of them, just one among many on the street. "I never thought a super assassin would get a hard on for a fast car."

"It sure beats trying to outrun the cops in a Hyundai." Herron smiled. "It really is unfair that a scumbag like Glennon gets around in a car like this."

She laughed as he pulled the car into the warehouse driveway, took it around back and parked. Kearns had found an ad for the place in a newspaper, while Herron had been busy with Glennon. It'd been for sale for years, so they were unlikely to be disturbed in the short time he planned to spend inside. He'd picked her up in the Mercedes and driven straight there.

"Wait here." He cut the engine. "This mightn't be pretty."

He was surprised when she nodded and left it at that. She clearly understood he needed to crack Glennon open to get to the secrets inside him. And, unlike when he'd been tortured by the brute at the compound, Herron knew exactly how to extract everything he needed from a person. He'd be disappointed if he didn't have the names he wanted in a few hours.

Herron exited the car and considered the rear of the warehouse. A large roller door dominated the front and there was a much smaller wooden door beside it. There appeared to be no security cameras or alarms, but that didn't mean much. Plenty of security measures could be hidden and if he had the time he'd have conducted a proper reconnaissance. He didn't have that luxury in this instance and brute force would have to do.

In Herron's experience, security was always flawed and a weak point could always be found. In this case, it was a good bet the warehouse owners would've secured the main roller door to prevent anyone making off with the warehouse contents. He doubted it they'd have been so diligent with the rest of the building. He reached the wooden door, took out his bump keys and the cheap lock opened with no trouble.

Herron drew his pistol and walked inside. The

warehouse was a giant, cavernous space with two doors leading off it. Whatever had been stored here had required four walls, a roof and not much else. Now it was empty. Herron checked the doors – one a janitor's closet, the other a bathroom, both unoccupied – then returned to the door he'd forced open, exited the building and walked to the car. Kearns was still in the car and she wound down the window as Herron approached.

"Stay here and keep an eye out." Herron took one last look around, to make sure they were alone. "I'll get our boy and head inside."

Herron walked to the back of the car and popped the trunk. From inside, Glennon peered out with red, frightened eyes. Herron couldn't blame him. He'd started the day on top of the world and ended it shoved into the trunk of his own car, with the prospect of the viral Armageddon that he and his co-conspirators had worked for at risk.

"Let's go." Herron waved the pistol so Glennon could see. "Climb out, slowly."

"What're we doing here?" Glennon's voice wavered.

Herron aimed the pistol directly at Glennon's head. "I'm not going to ask again."

Despite being handcuffed, Glennon managed to wrest himself out of the trunk. Once his feet were on the ground, Herron moved behind him and poked the pistol into his back. Glennon got the hint and they made their way inside. Herron forced him to sit on the concrete floor in the middle of the warehouse.

"I'm going to make this very simple." Herron crouched down to Glennon's level, but keeping enough distance between them to react if the other man lunged. "I know you bought smallpox from Fabian Bouchard and planned to infect the general population on World Environment Day. You and your collaborators injected yourselves with it. I want their names."

Glennon shook his head. "I'd rather die. The reckoning will proceed with or without me. Besides, you're not allowed to torture me on US soil."

Herron laughed and leaned in so that his face was only an inch from Glennon's. "Oh, those rules don't apply to me. I'm a sole contractor."

* * *

Herron gripped the rope tightly with both hands and pulled on it, grunting as Glennon's weight dragged on the other end. Glennon was already stripped to the waist and he screamed as he was raised feet first, until he suspended in mid-air with his head about three feet off the ground. Herron's makeshift winch wasn't perfect, but it had done the job. Herron had Glennon right where he wanted him

"There you go." Herron tied the rope off through the steel handle for the roller door and then stepped back to consider his handiwork. "Ready to talk?"

"Fuck yourself!" Glennon's face was already

flushed red and the vitriol he'd been spewing at Herron while he worked had only made it worse.

Herron shrugged. It was time for him to go to work. As well as a length of rope strong enough to hold Glennon's weight, he'd also found a broom, a bucket and a selection of cleaning chemicals in the janitor's closet. Herron started his prep, snapping the broom so he could use the handle as a weapon and filling the bucket with bleach. He hefted the broomstick and pushed the bucket closer to Glennon with his foot.

Without another word, Herron gripped the length of broom handle and swung it as hard as he could at Glennon's torso. The hanging man screamed in pain as the wood connected with his naked chest, but Herron didn't let up. He pounded Glennon over and over, taking his frustration out on the other man's upper body. Though he knew this was just the warmup, he hit the places that'd cause the most pain and zeroed in on the spots that guaranteed the loudest screams.

"Give me the names!" Herron shouted as he pounded Glennon, like a baseball hitter practicing his swing. "Give me the *fucking* names!"

Herron's efforts elicited shrieks and pleas, but no names. He took a step back and tossed the broom handle to the floor in disgust. Each second he spent here was time wasted. He poked the bucket with his toe, making sure it was lined up exactly under Glennon's head, then walked to where he'd tied off the rope. He untied the knot, braced himself to take

Glennon's weight and then lowered his captive's head towards the bucket full of chemicals.

"No!" Glennon screamed and thrashed. "No!"

"Last chance!" Herron paused the descent, but when Glennon didn't spill he kept going.

Glennon let out a curdling scream as his head descended into the bucket full of chemicals, followed by coughing and spluttering as his nose was submerged. Herron kept Glennon's mouth out of the liquid, so that he could speak if he needed to, but that was the only hint of mercy. He left the top half of Glennon's head submerged for about 20 seconds, then pulled on the rope and raised him out of the chemicals.

"Again?" Herron gritted his teeth against the strain of holding up Glennon's weight. "It can still get a whole lot worse."

"Go and fuck yourself!" Glennon hissed at him. His eyes were squeezed tightly shut and his face was bright red.

Herron sighed. In his experience, most people without training break incredibly quickly once the torture starts, but Glennon might well be a different beast. He lowered Glennon's head into the bucket again, earning more screams and energetic thrashing. He repeated the process four more times, but it proved useless.

Herron pulled on the rope and secured Glennon in place. His prisoner was still sputtering and his eyes were streaming, the pain likely overwhelming. After resting for a moment, Herron wiped his brow with the back of his forearm and then gripped Glennon's left pinkie finger and snapped it back violently. Glennon screamed loudly as it broke, denying Herron the satisfaction of hearing the crack.

Herron took a step back. "There are 206 bones in your body. I'm going to break one every 30 seconds until you tell me what I need to know. That's 103 minutes of the purest agony."

Glennon cursed some more, but Herron still didn't hear any names. He counted down from thirty and then repeated the process on Glennon's right pinkie. This time his prisoner tried to resist, clenching his fingers into a fist, but a swift punch in the balls got his hands loose again. Herron didn't talk any more. He simply worked on Glennon's fingers, counting down for each. Then he started on the toes.

When Herron was on the third toe of the left foot, Glennon finally broke and started to rattle off names. Despite thinking he'd triumphed, after only a moment Herron let out a long sigh. The problem with torture is that the victim will say anything to stop the pain, and there was often no way to tell the difference between truth and lie. Often, but not always.

Herron leaned in close to Glennon, his eyes narrow. "I know when you're lying and when you're telling the truth. Now, the *real* names, please."

Glennon sobbed as Herron resumed his work. Glennon screamed the same names — the lies — all the way through the rest of the toes on the left foot and half of the toes on the right. Herron didn't really plan to break all Glennon's bones. It would take too much effort. He had another idea in mind. He finished on the right foot, then took a step back.

"You're really going to make me do something I don't want to do, aren't you?"

Glennon was broken in so many ways, but he still wasn't giving up the names. "What?"

Herron dug into his pocket and pulled out Glennon's cell phone. He'd taken a moment earlier to scan through the text messages and learn that Glennon had a girlfriend – a woman named Michelle. From reading their last few messages, it was clear she planned to fly out of the country in less than a day. Glennon had probably orchestrated her departure to save her from the virus.

Herron typed a message into the phone, reading it aloud as he did so. "Hi, Michelle. I've had a car accident. Can you come pick me up? I—"

"What are you doing?" Glennon's voice had an edge of panic. "You leave her alone! She's done nothing to you!"

Herron stopped typing and fixed Glennon with a hard gaze. "You won't answer my question, so I'm getting your lovely lady along to help me."

"You leave her alone!"

"Heard you the first time." Herron went back to typing, but kept talking to Glennon as he did. "While she's on her way, I'll finish breaking your bones. Then I'll start on hers. You'll watch."

Glennon cracked like an egg. He spewed the names faster than Herron could check them off against the list from the compound, but he confirmed each and every one of them. Then, when Herron asked for physical descriptions, Glennon provided them. By the time he was done, Herron knew which fanatics he'd killed and, more importantly, which ones still needed killing and what they looked like.

From the hundreds of men in America with their names, he'd be able to narrow it down and find the ones who needed killing: Timothy Samuels, Shannon Mitchell and Mike Freeman.

"That wasn't so hard, was it?" Herron smiled. "If you'd been honest with me from the start, you'd be in a lot less pain right now."

"You'll leave Michelle alone now?" Glennon choked back tears, a man who'd totally betrayed his cause.

"Sure. It's time for you to go, though."

Herron turned his back on Glennon, walked to where the rope was tied and started to lower Glennon into the bucket. For a man intent on spreading viral Armageddon and killing millions, Glennon was very opposed to the prospect of dying. Herron watched impassively as he screamed and thrashed, but once his head was submerged it was over quickly.

"144."

Herron finally let go of the rope and flexed his fingers, which were sore after having to hold the Glennon's weight for so long. Glennon's body slammed into the concrete and contorted unnaturally, its head still in the bucket.

Whistling a soft tune, Herron turned and exited

the warehouse, his latest kill already out of his mind and replaced with considerations for tracking down the next threats. Killing Bouchard had ensured the supplier of the Omega Strain was unable to sell it again and now Herron had started to work on the carriers. Now he needed to find the rest of them.

Outside, Kearns was leaning against the Mercedes with her arms crossed over her chest and with a small plastic gas can sitting at her feet. "Well?"

"Time to go." Herron smiled at her, hoping there wouldn't be a repeat of the argument after he'd offed Bouchard. "No lecture about killing him?"

"He was going to die anyway." Kearns picked up the gas can and held it out to him. "You need to burn the body."

Herron frowned, looked down at the gas can and then back at her face. If she was telling him to burn the body, there must be a scientific reason for it. "Where'd you get the gas?"

"I went to the gas station."

Herron hesitated. He wanted to criticize her for going out in public without him, risking attention from the authorities, but he left it. Things between them had only just been repaired and he didn't have the time to waste arguing with her. If the bodies did need to be burned, then this part of his job wasn't done yet.

He took the gas can from her and walked back inside.

* * *

Herron parked the Mercedes at the same motel they'd stayed at the night before, just as dusk was settling in. Even after he killed the engine, Herron remained behind the wheel, gripping it so tightly his knuckles went white. Since the ambush at the compound, Herron had only had time to act, not think. Now he had a list of confirmed targets, he needed to work smarter. Only when Kearns cleared her throat next to him was he roused from his thoughts.

He turned to her. "What?"

She has a concerned look on her face. "Are you sure it's safe to come back here?"

"Safer than trying to book another motel with our details in circulation."

She still looked worried, but she nodded and they exited the car. Herron collected the backpack and followed Kearns to the same pair of motel rooms, already booked for several days using a fake name. Kearns was right in thinking that returning here after two homicides and a police chase was a risk, but given they'd only be here for a few quick hours of sleep, Herron was willing to chance it. It was the last opportunity they'd have to sleep. Tomorrow, he'd win. Then, he'd die.

Once he was inside his room, Herron put the backpack, car keys and pistol on the coffee table; his coins he left in his pocket. All he wanted to do was climb into bed and sleep, but he still had work to do. He did take a moment to stretch, though. His body was aching from a combination of physical exertion, the damage he'd taken at the hands of Copernicus and a lack of sleep. The few minutes of stretching did little for his aching muscles, but plenty for his mind. He began to formulate a plan.

He climbed up off the ground, stuffed the pistol down the back of his jeans and made sure he still had his room key in his pocket. He didn't relish what he was about to do, but he had no choice. He left his room, locked up and knocked softly on Kearns' door. It felt like a repeat of the morning, when he'd bashed on her door prior to them departing to take out Bouchard. He hoped she was still awake, but even if she wasn't he was going inside.

A few moments after he'd knocked, she eased the door open and peeked out. Only her face and eyes were visible. "What is it? I need to get some sleep."

"I need to come in for a moment." Herron took a half-step forward, making it clear that he wasn't going away. "We need to talk."

Her eyes flashed with suspicion. For a moment, Herron thought she might refuse his request, and he reached behind his back for the pistol. After a second or two, however, Kearns relented and opened the door. He let his hand fall to his side and stepped inside.

Kearns was still dressed, but she'd let her hair out and the lights were off except for the bedside lamp. It was clear she'd been about to climb into bed. Herron leaned against the wall while she closed the door and sat on the sofa.

He spoke once she was settled. "What you said

about the virus back at the warehouse got me thinking. I need to know what happens to me once the time comes."

She looked at him strangely for a moment, then curled up and hugged her knees. "It's not going to be great."

"I need to know *exactly* what'll happen. I'm planning to end the threat by killing the three carriers. I'm a fourth, though, and I need to figure out what to do."

She nodded. "You'll get a rash on your body and in your mouth and throat. It'll worsen and turn into fluid-filled blisters. The blisters will be small at first. As they grow, it'll get worse."

"Regular smallpox does that. I need to know what's different between this strain and the traditional ones. I need to know how long I'll have before I'm infectious."

She blinked a few times, confused. "You're fine in the prodromal stage — that's now — but from the time the rash appears you're going to be highly contagious. This strain will also have a more damaging effect on the body and be spread more easily. Anyone close to you after the rash appears is vulnerable."

"So this needs to be wrapped up before then?" Herron pushed himself off the wall. "I need to eradicate the carriers before the blisters appear and then kill myself?"

She shook her head. "Smallpox can live on in a corpse, that's why you needed to burn Glennon. Of all the viruses that stay around in the body after death, smallpox is one of the most viable. You need to burn it or freeze it to stop continued contagion. If you don't, you'll just ensure the poor schmuck who finds the bodies catches it."

"So I'm better off killing myself with fire." Herron reached behind his back and drew the pistol. "Thanks. That's all I need to know."

"What the fuck?" Kearns' eyes widened and she pushed herself back into the sofa.

Herron flipped the pistol in his hand and held it out to her by the barrel. "Take this."

Kearns' fear was replaced by confusion. "What are you doing?"

"Preparing you. You need to be ready to take the necessary action if the rash appears."

Fear flashed back across her face. "How did you—"

"How did I what?"

"Nothing." Her look changed instantly and she grabbed the pistol. "Won't you need this?"

Herron shrugged. "I've a spare. Now get some sleep. We're leaving early."

He left Kearns on the sofa cradling the pistol. Though she'd be able to sleep for a while, he wasn't ready to. Outside, he crossed the street and walked until he found a pay phone, about four blocks away. He dug in his pocket for enough coins to feed it, then dialed a number he'd committed to memory a decade ago – the number of a man whose life he'd spared.

"Hello?" The voice that answered the phone sounded tired and cautious.

"It's your old friend from Hong Kong." It was a phrase they'd agreed to a long time ago.

There was a long pause, which Herron had expected. It wasn't every day that an assassin who'd saved you a lifetime ago called and asked for a favor. Usually Herron could use the assets of his handler to get what he needed, but that door was closed. Now, he had to rely on secret supports he'd built up in a profession where life could end and friends could become foes at any moment.

He was speaking to the most valuable support of all. "I've some names and physical descriptions. I need you to find them."

7

HERRON PUSHED the door to the small internet café open, a chime sounding his arrival. The bored teen seated behind the counter didn't even look up from his cellphone. He was probably earning five bucks an hour working the graveyard shift when only gamers, stoners and those who couldn't afford a Verizon plan entered his world.

Kearns was dozing in the car. Once again, he'd knocked on her door at 2:00 AM and, once again, she hadn't been impressed. While she'd showered, he'd called his contact. The man had located two of the three targets Herron had asked him to find – Timothy Samuels and Shannon Mitchell. They matched the description and both were in Texas. His third target, Mike Freeman, had yet to be located. Herron would worry about him after the others were dead.

Herron and Kearns had started driving at 2:30 AM, taking Glennon's Mercedes on its last journey.

They were six hours into the drive – in Birmingham Alabama – before Herron had pulled up outside the 24-hour internet café. There was one thing he had to take care of before he reached Samuels' location in Houston and it'd take some time to set up online.

Herron approached the counter and placed twenty bucks on it. "Will this cover me for a half-hour or so?"

The attendant nodded, took the twenty and placed an access card on the counter. "Clean up after yourself."

"I won't need to do that." Herron laughed. "Say, do you have a USB I could have? I'll let you keep the change."

The cashier reached under the counter and pulled out a plastic tub filled with old USBs. Herron thanked him, selected one in the shape of a bikini-clad woman and made straight for the machine furthest from the café's entrance. Though there was nobody else in the place, he wanted to be sure there'd be no attention on him. He sat at the machine, inserted the access card and waited as the computer unlocked and granted him access

Before he could hunt the rest of the fanatics, he needed more firepower. It'd been easy to crack Bouchard and Glennon using nothing except the pistols he'd stolen from the CDC security guards, but there was every chance the others would be tougher nuts to crack. They'd be alert, suspicious and armed. Given Herron couldn't just walk into a gun store and buy a weapon, the internet café would help him take a less traditional route to acquisition.

Herron opened a browser window, navigated to armslist.com and skimmed the pages. Under normal circumstances, he'd contact his handler if he needed any gear. That wasn't possible now. He had his own stashes of cash, weapons and ID across the country, but no time to divert to the nearest one. Thankfully, finding a firearm in America was the easiest thing in the world, so long as he was creative.

He refined the thousands of weapons available on the site to a few hundred that fit his search terms: suppressed pistols made by manufacturers he trusted. Then he created a bogus profile and fired off messages to the best options. Once he'd finished, he'd sent messages to 230 potential sellers. In each, he asked if the gun was available immediately and where they were located.

The response wasn't instant, so Herron busied himself with his next job. He logged into an email account that'd his contact had set up a few hours ago. When they'd spoken on the phone, Herron had been forced to remember the login and password and promise not to write it down. That was easy enough. He punched in the details, opened the inbox and smiled when he saw only one email sitting in the drafts folder.

He clicked it open and his mission stared back at him.

His contact had provided detailed bios and photos of the two fanatics he'd managed to track down, Timothy Samuels and Shannon Mitchell. Both were in Texas and now Herron had head shots for both. He plugged the USB into the computer and downloaded the information from the draft email onto it. He ejected the device, deleted the email, logged out of the account and went back to the gun site.

By now, he had a few dozen responses from sellers. He filtered through them, removing any sellers that said their weapons weren't available immediately and any that seemed crazy or too much trouble. It shrank the list down considerably. Herron tapped his foot impatiently. Though it was early in the morning, there was a steady stream of replies until he landed on one that fit the bill perfectly.

"Jackpot." Herron smiled. The seller was based just outside Houston and a silenced pistol that would fit the bill.

After chatting with him for a few minutes, Herron agreed to the purchase and told the man he'd be there in nine hours or so. He scribbled down the details, closed the web browser and stood. Buying the gun wouldn't require a huge detour, but he knew he had barely had any time to spare. He pocketed the USB and left the café, without bothering to acknowledge the cashier on his way out.

He reached the car and climbed inside. Kearns was still sleeping soundly and didn't stir when he started the vehicle and got them back on the road.

* * *

Herron eased his foot off the accelerator, checked his mirrors and pulled off Texas State Highway 288 headed for Sunnyside. It was a shame to have to slow the Mercedes down after he'd spent several hours enjoying its performance on the highways between Atlanta and Houston, but he had business to conduct. If all went to plan, he'd get one more shot at a long, fast drive before he had to dump the car.

He slowed the vehicle as he drove along the exit, then he took a left onto Reed Road and a right at Scott Street. Just like that, he was in one of the most dangerous neighborhoods in Houston, where citizens had around a 10 per cent chance of being the victim of violent crime each year. It was just the place for Herron to arm himself and was right on the way to where Samuels was located.

He drove down Scott Street. As he passed derelict houses and shops covered in boards or graffiti, anyone he saw stopped what they were doing and stared at the car. They would be thinking he was an idiot for driving the Mercedes into this part of town and wondering how long it'd take for him to be carjacked. Herron laughed at the thought and parked right outside the Baptist Church his seller had told him to watch out for.

He killed the engine, unbuckled his seatbelt and glanced over to Kearns. "Wait here. I won't be gone for long."

Her eyes were wide as she looked around. A group of tough-looking kids was hanging out the front of the church and eyeing off their car. "Is it safe?"

"Safer than where I'm going." Herron gestured with his chin toward the glove compartment. "The pistol I gave you is in there. Wave it around if they try anything."

She still didn't look convinced as she nodded, pulled the pistol out of the glove compartment and put it in her lap. "Don't take too long."

Herron got out of the car. A glance at the group of kids was all it took to send them a warning, but he had no idea if they'd heed it or not. They'd be stupid not to. He put his hands in his pocket, crossed the street and walked a hundred yards down Barberry Drive to the Kings Row apartments.

The apartment buildings were double-story, though each apartment only took up a single level. Inside one, his seller waited. Herron cut across the grass, walked up the stairs and found apartment six. He pounded on the door several times, stood back and waited. Several heavy-duty bolts were thrown from the other side. Dean Hatfield – the seller – was serious about his security.

Finally, the door opened and a large revolver pointed out. It was the sort of gun that'd burst Herron's head like a watermelon hit by a bazooka. Behind it, a man smiled. "What?"

Herron looked up from the barrel and into the eyes of the man holding it. He looked somewhere between a pimp and a biker. "Hatfield? I'm your buyer."

"You got it." Hatfield smiled. His gold tooth gleamed as he raised the revolver, stepped back from the door and gestured for Herron to enter. "Welcome to my store."

Herron nodded, stepped inside and waited as Hatfield locked the door behind them. A quick look around the one-bedroom apartment confirmed they were alone. The place was filthy, filled with junk and a musty smell, just the sort of place Herron had hoped he'd find. Hatfield directed him to the small, two-person dining table and he sat.

"Ground rules." Hatfield dropped into a chair opposite Herron and put the big revolver on the table. "Money first. Gun second. No questions third. No cops fourth. Clear?"

"Suits me." Herron smiled. "I'm here because I need it to be quiet. Do you have the piece we agreed on?"

Hatfield picked up his revolver, walked to the sofa and hefted a large duffel bag. He returned to the dining table, slammed the bag down and unzipped it. It was full of pistols and revolvers, dozens of them. All were pieces of junk and none of them were what Herron had discussed with Hatfield online.

Hatfield pulled out a snub-nosed revolver and held it out. "This thing is just the ticket for a guy like you."

Herron took it. It was old, rusted and he wasn't sure it'd work at all. He struggled to hide his disdain. "This isn't what we agreed on."

Hatfield cracked a smile as he aimed his own

revolver at Herron. It was a much larger, nastier piece than the snub nose. And it was loaded. "It's what you're buying, though."

Herron sighed. He was insulted Hatfield would try to screw him. It was a wonder some other customer hadn't blown him away yet, given the shit he was trying to pull. "How much?"

"A thousand bucks." Hatfield's gold tooth caught the light and gleamed. "Plus, an additional five hundred bucks in tax so you get out of here safely."

Herron nodded. "My cash is in my back pocket. Can I stand and get it without you getting jumpy?"

"Slowly." Hatfield nodded. "Then you can take your new best friend, fuck off and kill whoever you plan to."

Herron stood, reached into his pocket and pulled out the wad of bills. He counted out the amount Hatfield had demanded and held it out. The dealer's smile grew wider as he reached out and grabbed the cash. Once it was safely stowed, he delved into the bag and then tossed a zip-lock bag of bullets onto the table. Inside were half a dozen rounds that'd fit the revolver.

"Thanks." Herron pocketed the bullets and the snub-nosed revolver. "Can I get out of here now?"

"Sure." Hatfield held out a filthy hand, letting his large revolver hang slack by his side. He was relaxed now he had his cash. "Remember my terms?"

Herron nodded and gripped Hatfield's hand. He squeezed tight and applied as much force downward as he could. Hatfield snarled and stepped into the pain, trying to resist as he brought his pistol up. Herron ignored the gun as he crouched low, pulled Hatfield toward him and then delivered a brutal head-butt to Hatfield's jaw. The top of his head struck perfectly.

"Prick." Herron took a step back and kept clear as Hatfield collapsed to the ground, out cold. The big revolver clattered to the ground beside him and blood dribbled from his mouth.

Herron took Hatfield's revolver, emptied the bullets and threw the gun to the other side of the room. It was an impressive weapon, but no use to him. Too big and too loud. He wanted what he'd come here for and nothing else would do. He returned to the duffel bag and rummaged through it, but all it held was the same kind of old, rusted weapons as Hatfield had tried to sell him.

Herron looked around, trying to locate where Hatfield would stash his good stuff. Though the apartment was full of junk, it was small and sparsely furnished. There weren't many places to hide a small arsenal. He tossed the whole house and came up empty. There wasn't a gun to be found that wasn't in the duffel bag.

Hatfield groaned – he was coming around. Herron ignored him and kept surveying the apartment. His eyes narrowed. There was enough plastic take out containers scattered around the apartment to build a wall, which told him Hatfield didn't cook much. Herron smiled and glanced at the small oven. It had a tinted-glass door that revealed little on the other side.

He opened the oven and his smile grew wider. Inside there were a half-dozen excellent pistols, two of them with silencers. This was obviously Hatfield's premium product. The weapons inside the oven were like a brand-new Ferrari when compared to the shit inside the duffel bag. He took a silenced pistol and a few clips and tossed the snub-nosed revolver.

Herron gave Hatfield one more kick, then stepped over him and left the apartment.

* * *

"A trailer park?" Herron's gaze lingered on the row of identical letterboxes at the edge of the road. A sign above them read: *Houston Mobile Home Community*.

"This is the address." Kearns held out the piece of paper on which he'd scribbled Samuels' location.

"Shit." Herron had been hoping he'd find the first of his three targets in a house in a quiet suburban neighborhood. This was going to be more difficult.

He'd returned to the car after beating up Hatfield to find Kearns safe in the Mercedes. The thugs he'd eyed off at the church hadn't moved an inch and he hadn't had to waste more time messing them up. It had been barely a ten-minute drive to the trailer park in the southern suburbs of Houston. Now he was looking at it, if there was a less ideal place for one of his targets to be hiding, he couldn't think of one.

He pulled the Mercedes off the side of the road and turned into the park's driveway. If the number of letterboxes was any indication it was a small facility, but there were still way too many eyes and ears around for his liking. Samuels clearly planned to stay cooped up until it was time for the reckoning, at which point he'd go out into the community and become a walking biological nightmare.

Herron drove past the reception building. It was the middle of the morning and there was one member of staff inside, but they paid him no heed. The deeper he got into the park, the more run down the place looked and Samuels' address put him right at the back of it. Herron parked the Mercedes a few trailers down from the target one, gripped the silenced pistol and shared a long glance with Kearns.

"Be careful." She gripped his arm. "There's no point barging in there like Superman if you just end up dead."

Herron nodded. He didn't have the time to explain to her that it was all part of the job and that the job got everyone killed sooner or later. For him, it'd be sooner; less than a day. He popped the car door, climbed out, stuffed the pistol down the back of his jeans and walked the short distance to Samuels' trailer. There was an old Ford pickup out front that Herron recalled seeing at the compound. That probably meant Samuels was home.

The trailer was a small, with just one way in and one way out, rendering any form of surprise entry almost impossible. Instead, Herron climbed the single step and pounded on the door, keeping the other hand gripping the pistol behind his back. There was no sound from inside and nobody answered the door. Herron's eyes narrowed a little as the curtain over one of the few windows twitched.

He jumped off the step.

A single rifle shot boomed from inside the trailer as Herron hit the lawn and rolled. He came up quickly, aiming at the door to the trailer. It now had a hole in it, right where he'd been standing a moment ago, but it was still closed and there was no further sound from inside. Samuels was buttoned up tight, daring Herron to force the door knowing there was a rifle waiting to ruin his day on the other side.

Herron retreated to the Mercedes, never taking his pistol or his eyes off the trailer. He was outgunned and didn't have time for a siege. Already, other residents were peering out of windows or poking their heads outside, looking for the source of the gunshot. He opened the door, climbed inside and with the door still ajar he started the car.

"What're you doing?" Kearns asked, confused.

Herron smiled. "Get out and walk to the front of the park. I'll meet you near reception in five."

She nodded, got out and hid her pistol in the waistband of her jeans. The instant the door slammed shut, Herron shifted to drive and put his foot to the floor. Three hundred horsepower of German engineering propelled the car like a rocket ship. Herron didn't even have to steer. The car was pointed straight at Samuels' trailer and as it hit 60MPH, Herron dived out the open door.

He hit the ground hard and rolled as the sedan smashed into the trailer with a tortured squeal of metal on metal. The smash was followed by shouts and cries for help from around the park. By his estimation, Herron had maybe thirty seconds before things started to get problematic with the other residents.

He came up to one knee, his pistol already drawn and scanning the trailer for any sign of Samuels and his rifle. The speeding Mercedes had smashed into the trailer's chassis, bending it around the front of the car and tearing a gaping hole in the mobile home's aluminum wall. The force of the impact had even moved the trailer a little, gouging the dirt where its wheels had shifted.

With the siege broken by his impromptu torpedo, Herron advanced on the trailer. The door was now ajar and he fired three silenced rounds into it. The slight popping sound of the pistol was pitiful compared to the carnage he'd just unleashed, but the important thing was that no rifle shot boomed in response. Herron gripped the door and yanked on it. Its shitty lock gave way first time.

A strip of aluminum had penetrated Samuels' stomach and pinned him to the cheap velour seat he'd been sitting in. At least one of Herron's shots through the door had also hit him. He was still holding the rifle, but it was slack in one hand. When

Herron entered, Samuels tried to move, but all he managed was a cry of pain and a dribble of blood.

Herron fired a pair of rounds into Samuels' head. "145."

He glanced around the trailer. With Samuels dead, he needed something to take care of the body. He picked up a green plastic stove lighter and set fire to the musty old curtains, the tablecloth, Samuels' clothes and the shattered pieces of wood veneer that the crash had dislodged. Once he'd lit a dozen different parts of the trailer, he tossed the lighter onto the ground and walked away.

Back in the open air, a crowd of residents milled about. Herron scanned them for threats, but nobody challenged him. As soon as they saw him and his pistol, the people just got out of his way. He walked to Samuels' Ford pickup, never taking his eyes off the gawkers as he used his bump key to open the door and start the vehicle.

Only when the trailer was burning out of control did he climb inside and drive away.

8

Herron passed the cashier a Bruce Springsteen cap. "I'll take this one."

The teenager scanned the label and looked at Herron for the first time. "$39.99."

"No bag, I want to wear it now." Herron handed over the cash.

The teenager grunted, took the cash and handed back the change, which Herron stuffed into his pocket. Then he donned the cap, turned from the merchandise booth and fell into line with a horde of other Springsteen fans streaming into Cowboys Stadium. In less than an hour The Boss would take the stage. Herron had been surprised that his contact had tracked Mitchell here, but here he was. It made for another difficult kill.

As he approached the stadium entrance, Herron hoped the cap would hide his face from security cameras. Though he doubted his facial profile would be loaded into the stadium's facial recognition system, he didn't want to take any chances. He'd killed enough people and stolen enough vehicles in the past few days that anything was possible. Usually he'd never leave such a trail of destruction, but with a job to do and no time to do it, pragmatic had replaced careful.

He'd lifted a ticket from the back pocket of a fan amidst the crush and now joined the line to enter the stadium through the gate printed on the stub. He shuffled forward, through the security barrier and metal detector, which didn't make a sound. He'd had to leave his pistol with Kearns, knowing there was no chance of getting it inside. Past security, he scanned his ticket scanned and entered the stadium. At no point did he so much as look at a member of staff.

He was properly alone now for the first time since the compound. He'd left Kearns at a diner and told her to relax for a few hours. With so many people around and no cellphones, the risk of losing her was too great. The two of them had driven in Samuels' Ford pickup from Houston to Dallas, and upon arriving, a quick payphone call to his contact had told Herron where his next target would be that evening. Now he just had to find the man.

A glance around got him started. At any other time, Herron would've appreciated the sheer scale of Cowboys Stadium, but right now he was interested only in the security guard he spotted patrolling the main concourse. Herron followed him, dodging around other fans and keeping far enough back to arouse the suspicions of neither the guard he was stalking nor any colleagues who might be watching the stadium security cameras.

Herron followed the guard until he paused at a door, scanned his access pass and pushed through it into a restricted stairwell. Herron managed to catch the door before it closed, slipped through and shut it behind him. Instantly, the bustle of the stadium and its thousands of noisy fans vanished, replaced by the sound of a single pair of boots walking slowly upstairs. Herron chased after the guard, calling out until the security man turned and faced him.

"Hey, buddy, I think I took a wrong turn." Herron tried his best impression of a meathead fan. "Can you help me?"

The guard frowned and pointed back the way they'd come. "You're not supposed to be in here. Head back down and out the first door you hit."

"Umm." Herron took a few steps up toward the guard, dug through his pocket and pulled out his ticket. He held it out to show the guard. "My ticket says I'm on level three."

"I don't care if you're in the owner's box, pal, you can't be in here." The guard leaned in to look at Herron's ticket. "You need to—"

Herron delivered a sharp blow to his stomach, causing him to double over. He followed up with a firm shove and the guard fell back. "Where's the camera room?"

"Fuck yourself, pal." The guard growled through gritted teeth.

Herron gave him a hard slap to his cheek. He didn't want to hurt him too badly, but this guy needed to play ball. "Where's the camera room? Tell me and I'll leave you alone."

"Up these stairs. Two more flights." The guard's voice was strained. "It's no good to you though, its locked from the inside."

"I'll worry about that." Herron slowly eased the pressure on the man's throat. "Now, I'm going to climb off you and you're going to remove your uniform, okay?"

The guard looked like he might resist again, until Herron raised a fist. "Okay, okay. Just take it easy, man. What the fuck kind of crazy are you, anyway?"

"The best kind." Herron climbed up off the guard and readied himself in case the guard tried to do something stupid.

The second the guard was out of his blue shirt and black pants, Herron socked him in the jaw. He dropped, but Herron made sure to catch him as he fell. He eased the security guard to the ground, then he dug around in the man's pockets for his access pass. He found it, along with some plasticuffs, which he used to bind the guard's wrists behind his back. Then he removed his own t-shirt and used that to bind the guard's feet together.

Herron put on the stolen uniform – the clothes were a little big, but would do the job – then ran up two flights of steps in almost no time. At the top was a steel door with a security scanner and no other features. He had no real way of knowing if the guard had lied to him, except to see what was on the other side. Barging into the police staging area or something equally inconvenient would really put a dampener on his day.

He held the access card to the reader and the light on it flashed red. Rather than try again, he pounded on the door and gripped its handle. While he waited, he plastered on a smile, hoping the combination of friendliness and the stolen uniform would reassure whoever was inside that he belonged inside as well. There was a peep hole on the door, but Herron was sure he was also being watched on camera.

A few seconds later the handle turned in his loose grip. Herron tightened his grasp as soon as the door started to open inwards and gave it a sharp push, using all his strength. There was a cry of alarm from the other side and the resistance on the door slackened. Herron kept moving forward, until the door was open fully and he was standing over the guard who'd opened it.

He leaned down and took possession of the guard's pistol, while he was still stunned, then held the weapon on the man. The guard was small and didn't look like he was interested in a fight, unlike his colleague. Herron could work with that. He glances around the room proper. A bank of monitors acted as the command center for every security camera in the stadium.

Herron pushed the door closed. It was time to get to work.

* * *

"Come on, baby." Herron's eyes narrowed as he scanned the screens.

He'd used the bikini-woman USB to load the photo of Mitchell into the stadium's facial recognition system and now the cameras were searching for just one person in a stadium filled to bursting. They would scan each seat and every walkway, leaving very few areas untouched as they scoured the stadium for their assigned target. It was frighteningly easy.

He sat back and crossed his arms. He'd only been running the search for a minute, but it felt like a lifetime. Herron knew it was only a matter of time before Mitchell popped up, but time was something he was very short on. At any second, stadium security could find the guard he'd left bound in the stairwell or realize their surveillance center had been captured. If that happened, he'd have dozens of cops and security giving him a hard time and no obvious way out. There was no choice, though. This was the most efficient way to find Mitchell in such a huge crowd

Herron laughed at the thought of Mitchell sitting somewhere in the stadium, preparing to watch the concert with a beer in hand, his last pleasure before he spread the virus that he thought was his little secret. If he knew that a dangerous assassin was using hundreds of cameras to close in on him he'd probably shit his pants.

"Hey, pal!" The guard Herron had knocked over

had finally built up the bravery to speak. "You need to think about what you're doing here. You're breaking all sorts of laws."

Herron swiveled in his office chair and looked at him. He had bound the guard's hands with his own plasticuffs, but otherwise left him be. The room was restraint enough and Herron had made sure of that by using the console to lock the door completely. "I know exactly what I'm doing. Keep calm and you'll live."

The guard shrugged. He was no hero. "I'm getting seven bucks an hour to sit in this concrete box. You can do whatever the hell you like."

Herron grinned. "I was hoping you'd say something like that. Is there some way I can speed up the system search?"

The guard looked up at the monitors and then back at Herron. "Did you tell it to leave out the gender you're not looking for?"

"It can do that?" Herron frowned. "Show me. I'm looking for a man."

The guard nodded, climbed to his feet and walked to the keyboard that drove the system. Though his hands were bound in front of him he could still type and Herron kept a close eye on him lest he alert his colleagues or somehow lock the system. The guard appeared willing to cooperate. After a few moments, he hit enter and took a step back. Herron glanced up at the screen and smiled when he saw everything moving much faster.

"It found your man." The guard gestured at the screen a moment later. "Not far from here."

Mitchell was up on the screen, smiling like an idiot while he chewed on some peanuts. Herron scribbled down the seat and section number on a piece of paper, then looked at the guard. "That man is a threat to everyone living in Dallas. I'm here to stop him. Will you keep quiet?"

"If you leave me alone, I'll cut myself loose with some scissors and pretend you were never here. What do I care about some asshole you're after?"

Herron stared at him for a moment. Unlike his colleague outside, this guard hadn't tried to resist. If he could save himself a few seconds by leaving this man standing, it was worth the gamble. He nodded, moved to the console and unlocked the door. With one last look at the guard, he turned and made his way out of the surveillance room, pausing only to scoop up a spare set of plasticuffs and hoping the trust he'd placed in the guard wouldn't backfire.

Herron ran as fast as he could down the stairwell and through a door to the third-level concourse. He paused only briefly, to check the seat and section he'd written down against the stadium signs. Mitchell would be three rows around from him and it took Herron less than a minute to find the right section. He took the steps down the aisle two at a time, until he found Mitchell's seat.

Slowing to a walk, he leaned in to catch Mitchell's attention, ignoring any patrons who expressed concern about having a security guard appear. "Sir?"

Mitchell looked up, a little surprised. "Yes?"

"I'm pleased to tell you you've won a pre-concert meet and greet with Mr Springsteen." Herron was all smiles as he gestured to the concourse. "If you'd like to come with me..."

"Stop talking shit, pal." Mitchell scoffed. "I never entered any competition."

Herron's smile broadened. "Everyone who bought a ticket was entered into the draw. Your seat was selected as the winner."

Mitchell frowned, his natural suspicion clearly in a battle with his desire to meet Bruce Springsteen before he died. This was one complicated fanatic, that was for sure. If he didn't take the bait, the alternative would be much messier and much noisier. Finally, with a shake of his head, Mitchell climbed to his feet. Herron wasted no time, walking back up the aisle to the concourse with Mitchell on his heels.

His face turned away from Mitchell, he allowed himself a smile.

* * *

Herron fumbled for his stolen security pass, waved it against the card reader and opened the door. He gestured for Mitchell to follow him through. The secure staff walkway beyond ringed the entire stadium, connecting the food stores, bars and storerooms that served a hundred thousand people.

Admittance to this private area was enough that all the fanatic's remaining doubts dissipated.

As he strode around the concourse, leading Mitchell to his fake meeting with The Boss, Herron tried to figure out the best place to dispose of Mitchell's body. As his eyes darted around and read the signs on each door they passed, he gazed at one and an idea formed in his head. He wasn't sure he'd find what he needed on the other side, but it seemed like his best shot.

Herron turned and smiled at Mitchell. "Are you ready?"

Mitchell frowned. "This is a kitchen."

Herron's left fist was flying before Mitchell finished speaking. The punch connected with the fanatic's jaw, jerking his head around. Herron's fist exploded with pain, but the shot had the desired effect. Mitchell hadn't been expecting the blow, and his eyes went glassy and his knees went weak. As he fell, Herron caught his weight and dragged him through the kitchen's swing doors.

The kitchen was empty. He'd noticed signs on the doors along the utility walkway that indicated which kitchens and retail outlets were in use, and for some reason this small concession stand was closed for the concert. All it contained now was the apparatus to keep a stadium full of people in sodas and fried food. That suited Herron just fine – he didn't have to worry about being interrupted.

Fire and heat were Herron's first thoughts for dealing with Mitchell. He looked around and spotted the deep fryer, but it was switched off. He eased Mitchell's unconscious bulk onto the floor and inspected the fryer, but soon ruled it out. It would take too long to get hot and there were practical issues with placing a grown man inside a fryer, anyway. It didn't matter, because his eyes soon settled on another option.

A much larger, cooler option.

Herron hauled Mitchell in the direction of the large freezer that ran off the kitchen. The stunned man was beginning to stir, but it was easy enough for Herron to slide the door open and drag him inside, right to the back. Herron dumped him on the ground, then dug in his pockets for the spare plasticuffs from the security room. Once Mitchell's wrists were bound together behind his back, Herron hit him hard with a bag of frozen French fries, making sure he didn't come to in the next minute or so.

Now he had time to do the job properly. Herron returned to the kitchen, picked out a knife, returned to the freezer and eased the door closed behind him. The easiest thing in the world would have been to stab Mitchell, but given Herron couldn't get his body out of the stadium, he didn't want to risk spreading the man's contaminated blood.

Instead, he gripped the knife and used it to cut Mitchell's clothes off. His sweater, t-shirt and pants parted under to the sharp chef's blade and when Mitchell was in nothing but underwear, Herron tossed the knife onto the ground. He picked up the remains of Mitchell's t-shirt and used it as a gag, just in case the infected terrorist regained consciousness before he died. Then, quickly, he returned to the kitchen, found a notepad and pen, and scrawled a few words in large letters.

Back in the freezer, he admired his handiwork: he was quite proud of this one. The penultimate carrier was bound, stripped and unconscious in a commercial freezer. Kearns had said freezing the virus would work as well as burning it and Mitchell would freeze to death in almost no time. If his body was hidden well enough, the virus could be kept on ice indefinitely.

Gradually Mitchell was coming around and mumbling through the gag. "Mmmm!"

"This is what happens to assholes who try to wipe out humanity." Herron sneered at Mitchell as he dropped the note he'd written on the floor: *Biohazard. Contact the Center for Disease Control.*

After that, it only took a few minutes to surround Mitchell with enough boxes of frozen food that his body wouldn't be found for a week. Satisfied the fanatic was well hidden, Herron closed the door to the freezer room. The door was lockable, and the key still in place, so Herron turned it and then snapped it off. Anyone who wanted to open it would need a locksmith and a fair bit of time.

The last thing he did was turn the temperature down to -20 degrees. Now nothing could stop Mitchell freezing to death inside his dark tomb.

"146."

Herron returned to the walkway, one hand resting

on the pistol stuffed into the waistband of his pants. He walked half the circumference of the stadium, knowing exactly where he had to exit and planning only to return to the general concourse when he was near the right spot. A few staff members saw him as they headed in one direction or another, but ignored him. A man in uniform was invisible where people expected to see them.

A man wearing black pants, a polo shirt and a name badge smiled as he headed towards Herron from the opposite direction. Dimly, Herron recognized his face...

Then he drew his pistol and leveled at the man in black, just as the other man did the same to him.

9

"WALK AWAY." Herron's aim was locked on and he had the trigger half-squeezed. If the man in black made the slightest movement, he'd fire.

His name badge identified him as Walter and though he was dressed like a food attendant, he was nothing of the sort. He was a contractor. "You were told to give up on this job."

Herron swallowed hard. He had no answer. There was a code among the best professional killers, the few men who could do any job and take out any target. Herron had long lived by that code and he knew the deal: you don't piss in another contractor's patch. Except, in this case, he knew he was doing just that. He'd kept going when his handler had told him to stop and now he was preventing one of his colleagues from completing a job he'd been assigned.

"I won't ask you again." Walter's voice was calm

and reasonable. "You're interfering in a matter that no longer concerns you. I have it in hand."

Herron was at a red line moment. If he did anything except lower his weapon and walk away he'd be expelled from the ranks of his profession. He'd knowingly pushed his luck, backing himself to stay one step ahead of whoever his handler assigned to take care of the fanatics, but now that man had caught up with him. Walter was a wall that stood between him and completion of the job. He had to deal with it.

"It's my mission." Herron snarled. "Tell me where to find Freeman and leave it to me. You can tell our mutual friend you couldn't find him."

"That'd be a lie. I have found him. I'll be on my way to his house as soon as I find where you've stashed Mitchell."

"So we both have information the other needs. If we team up, we can do this with a lot less bloodshed."

"You know it doesn't work like that." Walter shrugged. "All right. No weapons and the first man to drop gives the other the answers he needs?"

Herron nodded, tossed his pistol aside, raised his fists and stalked forward. His opponent mirrored his actions. Each of them was more than a match for any other person on Earth, but against one another? Herron didn't know if he could beat Walter, but the opportunity to find Freeman meant he had to try. Walter would certainly talk if he lost, as would Herron, but their code meant the loser would also have to die, leaving the winner to continue with the mission.

They approached one another with their guards raised. Two trained killers with no time to lose... Herron was tired, hadn't eaten properly and was carrying other injuries, while Walter looked fresh. This had to be over quick, or else Herron was done for. He threw a series of quick, sharp jabs, all of which were blocked easily. He was searching for an opening, probing his foe, who responded with similar feints.

Then Herron found a way through. Walter lowered his guard slightly, a sloppy mistake from a confident fighter. Herron took a chance, aiming a shallow strike at Walter's head. It didn't land. Walter adjusted his guard faster than Herron had ever seen, deflected the shot and delivered a hard chop to the ear. Herron staggered and Walter didn't let up. Herron did his best to fend him off, but an elbow struck his temple and he staggered back a step.

Though he'd promised to tell the truth and abide his fate if he lost, he hadn't promised to fight fair. As Walter stalked forward for the kill, Herron lunged at him. With his right hand he feigned high, easily blocked. With his left, he grabbed Walter's testicles and squeezed. Walter gave a high-pitched whine and struck out, trying to get him to release his grip, but now Herron had an advantage he wasn't going to let up.

Herron took the small opening, knowing it might be the only one he got. He balled his fist and slammed it into the assassin's face. Walter let out a grunt as his nose was smashed, but Herron cursed as well when a bone in the mashed organ cut his hand. But the pain was irrelevant: he had the opportunity to win. He struck again, hurting his own hand even more but sending his opponent to the ground.

Herron wasted no time. He rushed over to his pistol, picked it up off the ground and aimed it at Walter. He then took possession of Walter's silenced pistol. "Where's Freeman?"

"Nowhere." Walter pushed himself up to a sitting position. He let out a laugh and shrugged. "He doesn't exist. It's a fake name."

"Bullshit." Herron hissed the words, outraged the other man would go back on his word. He knew Freeman existed. He'd met the man. "Where is he?"

"You're looking for a man named George Haskell. He's in Atlanta, back where all this started to go to shit for you." Walter shrugged. "Good luck with it."

Herron wanted to push him further, but he had the only answer he was going to get. Walter could be lying, but the name Haskell did ring a bell... and, if it was a dead end, there was always his contact who'd tracked down the other fanatics and might still do the same for Freeman. Herron had enough to go on with, so there was no point waiting around. Before he could proceed, though, there was one more thing to take care of.

As Herron looked down at him, Walter smiled up at him, teeth bloody but with no fear or hatred in his eyes. He knew he'd been bested and it was the end of the line, a point most people in their business reached sooner or later. Herron didn't say anything, he didn't need to. Two men couldn't work the same job and failure wasn't an option. Herron raised the silenced pistol and fired. Walter's body slumped to the floor.

"147."

* * *

Herron pushed open the door to the diner, wishing he had time to stop and drink a gallon of coffee and eat a dozen sandwiches. The place was deserted except for Kearns, sitting alone in the window booth furthest from the door where she could see everyone coming and going long before they could reach her. She'd learned something from him. She was smart.

If she was even smarter, she wouldn't be there at all. Herron had expected her to bail or call the cops, but it looked like she'd done neither. It proved to him that she might have a role to play in the end game. He made his way over, sat opposite her and ordered a coffee from a hovering waitress who made no comment about his bloody and bruised appearance.

Kearns wasn't so polite. She waited until the waitress left, then looked him up and down. "You look like shit."

Herron shrugged and leaned forward, speaking softly and choosing his words carefully. "The package is in a freezer. He should be dead by now. Will that do?"

Kearns nodded. It surprised Herron how quickly she had got used to the talk of death. "It's not ideal, but the virus won't be able to activate and spread while it's frozen."

"Good enough." Herron paused. He didn't want to tell her about the other assassin. "It was the best I could do."

"I should call in the CDC to deal with that one or else someone will eventually find it and this will all have been for nothing."

"Do it." He'd expected and planned for her to do exactly that when he'd stashed Mitchell in the freezer. "I need to make a call myself."

He explained where to find the freezer and the body inside it, then they stood and walked to the bank of payphones at the back of the diner. Herron took the phone as far as possible from Kearns, fed it some coins, dialed a number and held the receiver to his ear. At the end of this phone call, he'd either have the final piece of information he needed to destroy the Omega Strain or he'd have failed.

Finally, the call was answered. "Hello?"

Herron sighed with relief. "It's me. I assume you didn't find Freeman?"

"No…" The voice trailed off. "How'd you know?"

Herron cursed. It meant Walter had told the truth. "He doesn't exist."

"Nope. There's no man named Mike Freeman alive who matches your description."

"Okay. Find George Haskell for me instead. I'll call back in an hour."

Herron hung up the phone and took a second to compose himself. All this time chasing after Freeman and now his target had changed. It wasn't an ideal situation. The reckoning was close but now Herron wasn't sure who it would be with. Still, the name George Haskell nagged at him, like having a word on the tip of his tongue or hearing a song he knew well but couldn't name.

He returned to his table and sat with his head in his hands, chewing over the name in his head. The waitress placed a coffee cup in front of him, but he left the beverage untouched. He kept an eye out for Kearns, keen to be off as soon as she was done but without knowing where he needed to go. She took another five minutes on the phone and then returned to where they were seated.

"I've told the CDC about the body." She smiled. "It's all good. They'll take care of it as soon as they can get a team in place."

"Great." Herron forced a smile, but couldn't pull it off. "Freeman doesn't exist. We're after another man. His name is familiar, but I can't place it. George Haskell..."

"What?" Kearns' expression wouldn't have been much different if Herron had slapped her. Her eyes went as wide as dinner plates.

In the last few days Herron had seen her handle dead bodies, car chases and a terrorist plot with less reaction than this single name had just caused her. "What?"

"I was just on the phone to him." Her voice was barely above a whisper. "Haskell is the head of the Center for Disease Control."

"Motherfucker." It fell into place. Herron knew exactly where he'd seen the name now: on a plaque in the lobby of the CDC building in Atlanta.

There'd been no way he would ever have linked the name to Freeman. Until now.

"You need to call someone else you trust at the CDC and get them to clear the body, Erica." Herron paused. "I think your boss has other things on his mind."

* * *

Herron winced as he pulled the plain black jacket on over a white t-shirt, both of which still had their tags attached. He looked at himself in the mirror and shrugged. Back at the diner he'd used the public bathroom to tidy himself up, washing the blood off his hands and cleaning his face, but the uniform he'd stolen from the security guard had been too damaged to wear any longer.

With Kearns, he'd climbed inside their stolen Ford pickup and driven straight into Downtown Dallas. Herron had parked outside a bank, sent Kearns to buy a burner phone and walked right into the bargain clothing store a few doors down. The new threads up top combined with the new jeans down below wouldn't win any fashion awards, but they were better than his old clothes.

"How are you for sizes in there, sir?" The cheery sales assistant on the other side of the change-room curtain had flitted around him since he'd entered the store.

"Fine." Herron switched his possessions into the pockets of his new jeans, then stuffed the pistol down the back of them and opened the curtain. "How much?"

"An even thirty dollars, sir." The sales assistant spoke earnestly. Given the state he'd been when he'd walked in, she probably though he was a hobo.

Herron dug in his pocket and pulled out a small wad of notes, the last of the cash he'd picked up along the way. He held a fifty out and the woman's look changed. "Keep the rest."

From entering the store to leaving it had taken less than six minutes.

The sky outside was gloomy and threatening rain. He walked towards where the truck was parked, but seeing Kearns still wasn't back yet, he continued into the bank. If there was a contrast to the no-frills clothing store he'd just been in, the opulence of a big city bank was it. The place stank of money.

In his fresh, cheap clothes Herron approached the information counter and waited in the line. There were dozens of customers either finishing their business ahead of him or joining the queue behind, but it wasn't long before he was at the front of the line. One of the three staff behind the information counter finally smiled at Herron, signaling he should step forward.

"Good afternoon sir, how can I help you today?" The bank employee's hands hovered over his keyboard.

"I was mugged earlier and had my wallet and identification stolen." The lies rolled off Herron's tongue easily. "I need access to my deposit box. My name is Mitch Daniels."

"I see." The banker was slightly taken aback, as if in shock at the thought of someone dressed so cheaply being able to afford a deposit box. "Let me check for you, Mr Daniels."

Herron waited while the banker entered the name into the computer and wasn't surprised at all when the other man's smile grew from professionally polite to seriously delighted. Having a few million dollars in cold, hard cash deposited in the bank tended to have that effect on its staff. The employee looked up at Herron and then down at the computer once more, no doubt checking his photo.

"Please accept my apologies that you had to wait in line, Mr Daniels." The banker nodded once. "I'll hand you off to my branch manager now. Have a good day."

"Have a good day yourself." Herron switched his attention to the man's boss, an older woman. "Howdy."

"Nice to meet you, Mr Daniels. We'll take care of you right away." The bank manager was prim and proper, but seemed less inclined to smile. "Follow me."

Herron nodded and followed her through the public areas of the bank and into the much more secluded area where rich people kept rich people things. Given he'd been handed off to her by a member of staff, the bank manager did nothing so crass as to ask him for identification. Though his fake name and photo might have got him past the first gate, only one thing mattered deeper into the bank.

"Wait here a moment, please." The bank manager continued a few steps forward, entered a code into a keypad, pushed a heavy steel door open and glanced at Herron. "This way, sir."

Herron walked after her and once inside took a moment to survey the room. Apart from a very large hardwood table in the middle of it, the only other feature was hundreds of steel safety deposit boxes lining the walls. They were a range of sizes, the one Herron owned being in the middle of the range. It was about the size of a hardcover novel.

"I have box 381," Herron said.

"Very well."

She pulled back a panel on the ornate hardwood table, revealing a touchscreen, then punched in Herron's three-digit box number. She took a step back, allowing Herron to lean in and enter a ten digit code of his own. The screen went green.

"Excellent." The bank manager entered another ten digits. "I shall leave you to your box. Just come out when you're done."

"Thanks." Herron while she exited, leaving him alone with nothing but his thoughts and the accumulated wealth of Dallas' rich and famous.

He walked to the small door behind which his box was housed. It was now unlocked, and he opened it, removed the metal box and returned to the table. He spun the small dial on the box to the correct combination and opened the lid. Inside the box was a smorgasbord of the finest items a contract killer would need for a life on the run.

Without delay, he pocketed his fake ID and wads of rolled-up cash. He left the pistol, the bulk of the money and a USB drive in the box and then closed the lid, locked the box and returned it to its place behind the security door. In little more than a minute after the bank manager had left him alone in the room, he was ready to follow her out.

Ready for the final act.

10

HERRON DROVE WELL below the speed limit as he approached Haskell's house. The late afternoon sun was shining bright but the trees lining both sides of the road ensured there was plenty of shade for the expensive European cars parked underneath. Herron's old, stolen sedan was out of place, but that wasn't an issue. Once he parked the vehicle he never intended to return to it.

After Kearns had returned to the pickup truck with the phone, Herron had driven it and dumped it at Dallas Executive Airport, a small regional airport 10 miles out of the city. It handled small passenger planes, private planes and cargo aircraft. During the drive, he'd called ahead, booking two seats on a charter from Dallas to Atlanta.

His fake ID had worked to get him aboard, while a wad of cash on top of the ticket price had been good enough to get Kearns aboard with no questions.

Herron had told the pilot that she was his mistress and there needed to be no paper trail. The man had understood completely, welcomed them aboard and even rustled up a bottle of champagne from when he'd had Cher as a passenger a week earlier. The pilot hadn't even put them through a security screen, letting him take his pistol aboard.

They'd landed at a small airport just outside of Atlanta, as per the pilot's original flight plan. After thanking the pilot and giving him another wad of cash to ensure his silence, Herron and Kearns had left the airport, stolen a sedan and hit the road. It had been less than an hour's drive to Haskell's home, directed by Kearns, who'd visited her boss there once before.

"Looks quiet." Herron gazed at the house. It had looked the same the last three times they'd driven past – a modest home for a man of Haskell's position, a simple red brick house with a nice lawn. Herron couldn't see any security features, which was strange for a fanatic intent on unleashing a pandemic on the world.

Kearns said nothing. She was still in shock that her boss was the mastermind of the Omega Strain and had been withdrawn during both the flight to Atlanta and the drive that followed. Herron didn't push the issue. Instead, he parked half a mile down the street and prepared to strike. Though he didn't like that it was broad daylight, he didn't have time to wait for darkness before making their move.

The virus could start to act at any moment.

He turned to face her. "You stay here."

She shook her head. "Not a chance. I haven't come this far to sit in the car for the end."

She had a point. Haskell's goons had kidnapped her and their work was a direct insult to hers. Herron respected the choice she'd made to follow him into danger one final time. She wouldn't be dead weight, either; her scientific knowledge might prove useful and she'd already agreed to take Herron out if the virus became active and he was incapacitated.

"Let me secure Haskell first, then I'll come get you. That okay?"

"Fine." She nodded.

He got out of the car, reached into the vehicle for his pistol and stuffed it down the back of his jeans. Then he walked in the direction of Haskell's house. It felt strange to be walking to the site of his final kill, the last mission Herron would finish before his own death, but he filed the thoughts away. He couldn't afford a hint of distraction or emotion.

He paused when he reached the house two down from Haskell's place, then turned and walked up the driveway, taking the side path to the back of the house. He scaled the fence and dropped into the backyard, and was halfway across the yard when his luck ran out. A deep growl made him wince and he looked around to find its source – a large German Shepherd standing on its dog bed.

Herron ran. The second he moved, the dog let out a loud and aggressive bark. Herron sprinted for the fence, reached it in ten long strides and jumped, pulling himself up and drawing his legs in close to his torso. It wasn't enough. The dog jumped at him, clamping its jaws down on his left leg. Herron winced and it took all his willpower to swallow the pain and not cry out.

He kicked out at the dog. The beast's weight dragged him down from the fence, and he kicked out with his right foot multiple times. Each blow seemed to make the dog more determined to hang on. With a growl of his own, Herron let go of the fence and let his bodyweight fall on top of the dog. It wasn't graceful, but it was effective. He landed hard. The dog let out a yelp of pain and its jaw unlocked.

Herron seized his chance, scrambling to his feet and up onto the fence again. This time the dog was too slow to move and Herron was up and over the fence before it could bite him. He made dropped down onto the grass in the backyard of Haskell's house, glad the dog hadn't slowed him down too much.

At Haskell's back door, drew his pistol and eased the door open. He couldn't see anyone, but there were muffled voices coming from the front of the house. He stepped inside, moving quietly through the house, taking the time to check each room, pistol probing wherever his eyes looked. As he moved forward, the voices grew louder.

"...it's wonderful to see you safe after being kidnapped by that madman." Haskell's voice dripped with sarcasm. "You were stupid to come here."

"Please, put the gun away!" Kearns' voice was

filled with panic. "I just came here to warn you about a virus I've found!"

Herron's eyes widened. He had no idea why Kearns was in the house, but everything had just got harder. He rushed to the front of the house, bypassing rooms on the way – it was sloppy practice, but he had to get to Kearns quickly. He turned the corner with his pistol raised, but things had already gone to shit. Haskell had a pistol to Kearns' head and his forearm wrapped around her throat.

"Mitch! I'm sorry! He grabbed me from the car!" There was fear in her eyes, unmistakable. "Shoot him!"

Herron was confident he could make the shot, but he couldn't risk a reflex action from Haskell killing Kearns. "Put it down, Haskell. It's over. Your carriers are dead."

"Au contraire." Haskell laughed. "There are four carriers in this house, not just you and I."

Herron frowned. Who else?

Herron grunted as something hit him hard in the back of the head. The pistol fell from his hand and he dropped to one knee, trying to turn and face his new attacker. A woman stood there, meat-tenderizing mallet raised to strike him again. He must have missed her when he rushed to the front of the house.

As the closest physical threat, this woman had to be dealt with before he could help Kearns. He lunged and tackled her, his shoulder driving into her midsection as he took her to the ground. She grunted and the wind escaped her, the mallet clattering to the wooden floorboards. They struggled for a moment, but it was no contest. Herron had the training, the strength and the leverage to best her.

Herron rolled on top of her, half expecting Haskell to shoot him at any moment. But the sounds of a struggle behind him told him Kearns was keeping her captor busy, buying him time. He reared up and lashed out with his fist, catching the woman in the jaw. She fell to the ground and her head hit the floorboards hard.

"Mitch!"

Herron turned towards the cry. Haskell had tightened his chokehold on Kearns and was pointing his pistol at Herron. Pressing his attack on the mystery woman would mean sacrificing Kearns, and even then Herron wouldn't be able to deal with Haskell before the man simply shot him. He was outgunned, out of position and out of time.

He'd failed.

"You're out of luck." Haskell seemed to read his mind. "Get off my wife, lay face down on the ground and put your hands behind your head."

Herron knew he was fucked. He'd lost the pistol in the struggle and Haskell had the advantage. All he could do was comply and hope there was another chance to strike later. He did as Haskell instructed and climbed off the woman, who was out cold, blood trickling from her mouth. That was little consolation to Herron as he lay face down, locked his fingers behind his head and waited.

Kearns cried out in pain, but Herron kept still. If

he was going to get another chance, he needed to pick his moment. Haskell stalked closer, his footfalls heavy on the wooden floor. Herron listened hard, waiting for precisely the right moment. He didn't even move when Haskell kicked him hard in the midriff or when Kearns started to cry – the realization that they'd lost must have finally hit her.

Herron was about to spring into action and strike when a blow hit him square in the jaw. Herron grunted as his head snapped around. The last thing he heard before he blacked out was Erica Kearns calling his name, desperation in her voice.

* * *

"You killed my wife, you know?"

Herron blinked and focused. He was in some sort of home lab. Science equipment lined the stainless-steel benches and Herron wondered how much of the work to develop the Omega Strain had occurred here. Haskell stood nearby, wearing the smile of a man who knew he'd won, and Herron could understand why. He was in bad shape and his right hand was bound to the leg of a camp stretcher. He glanced at Kearns and she was also restrained and looking dejected.

Herron looked back at Haskell. "You don't seem upset about it."

Haskell shrugged. "She was going to die in a few days anyway. Same as you and me."

"You infected her as well?" Herron shook his head.

"Everyone has to make sacrifices, my family included. My wife was as committed as I."

"You're a monster." Herron had no family, but even if he did he couldn't imagine injecting them with a death sentence.

Haskell shrugged and returned to his work. The conversation seemingly over, Herron took the opportunity to test out his restraints – though the bed was light, just canvas over an aluminum frame, he couldn't achieve much by dragging it across the room by his wrist. Kearns would be no help either, just sitting there staring into space. There was only one way out of this mess: Haskell himself.

"Nice lab you've got here." Herron tried again, but this time he was speaking to Haskell's back. "Looks expensive."

Haskell laughed and kept working. "You'd be amazed at how much high-end gear the CDC throws away and how easy it is to divert deliveries from the dump to another location. Every piece of gear in here would've gone to landfill, when they're perfectly good. It is just another example of the environmental destruction we're responsible for."

"So you spend your days working to prevent the spread of contagions and your nights working to develop and spread the most dangerous one on the planet?"

"Yes, yes." Haskell waved a hand as he leaned over a microscope. "We keep nature from attacking humanity with its viruses and diseases. In return, humanity rapes and exploits and pillages nature, never content with what it has and always wanting more. I've spent my life at the crossroads of these things and when I realized the problem I had to act."

Herron tuned out Haskell's rant and tested his restraints again. The thin cord that'd been used to bind his wrist to the camp bed was tight, although it did have some give. With time, he might be able to free himself, but time was running out. At any moment the virus could go from being latent to active.

"I wouldn't bother trying to escape." Haskell's turned from the microscope to face him. "Even if you get free of your restraints, we're sealed in here. Nobody gets out unless I say so."

"I wouldn't be so sure. You said the same thing at the compound, yet here I am." Herron gave his restraints one last jerk.

Haskell laughed. "I could have killed you there, but instead I left you alive and made you into a carrier. Your presence here is completely immaterial. You didn't think I'd simply be waiting in my house, like a plump chicken ready to be slaughtered? I know you've taken out my other carriers, which isn't ideal, but it hasn't really impacted my plans."

Herron scoffed. "I took out your designer and your lemmings. There's no way to get the spread you need."

"You're wrong. I only ever needed one carrier..."

Haskell walked over to Herron and leaned in close. "Me."

Herron jerked forward and tried to head-butt Haskell, but the scientist backed away. Herron grinned. "Close."

"Not close enough." Haskell took another step back. "The virus is so fucking beautiful that one point of infection will more than do the job. More carriers were always a bonus and the three of us here are more than enough to spread the virus and cleanse the stain of humanity from the Earth."

Herron frowned. "Three?"

Haskell's face clouded over with confusion. Then realization set in. "Oh, you poor fool. She hasn't told you?"

Herron's eyes shot to Kearns. She stared back at him emptily. Herron clenched his teeth hard. He'd been played for a fool. Though he'd rescued Kearns from the compound, he'd never spent much time discussing her captivity. There'd been a few hints, but he'd never put it together that she was carrying the virus. He'd been racing to kill all the carriers and then end himself, when a carrier had been beside him the whole time.

Kearns spoke after a moment. "They injected me at the compound, too. Why'd you think I was so keen to stay on this ride with you? I wanted to help you end it."

"Well, I guess we're screwed then." Herron kept his eyes on her for a long second, but kept his face impassive when she winked. Then he jerked forward again, dragging the camp bed and lunging at Haskell. "I'm going to fucking kill you."

Haskell sighed as he grabbed a pistol from the counter and aimed it at him. "Didn't you listen? You're dead either way and there's no way out."

Herron closed his eyes, ready for the end if it came, but hoping his gamble had paid off. He could see the barrel of the pistol trembling in Haskell's hand, which gave him some hope that he'd distracted Haskell enough. He was playing Russian Roulette and every chamber of the gun was loaded.

Herron winced as the pistol fired, the explosion blasting his ears, then he snapped into action. He jumped to his feet and dragged the bed towards Haskell, who was struggling with Kearns on the floor. She'd freed herself and tackled Haskell as he fired, causing the shot to miss. They'd gone to ground and now he was laying punches into her.

Herron joined the fray, though he only had one free hand and the bed was dragging behind him. Haskell grunted as Herron landed on him, but then managed to shuffle away from the confrontation. Herron kicked out at him and connected firmly with his chest. Though the scientist cried out in pain, it wasn't enough. Haskell increased the distance between them in seconds. Kearns was still recovering from the hits she'd taken and Herron was ineffective now.

"You're both wasting your time!" Haskell hissed as he scurried over to the metal bench and grabbed the silenced pistol he'd taken from Herron, his own still on the floor.

Herron watched, unable to do anything as Haskell turned and aimed the pistol at him at the same moment as Kearns reached for the pistol on the ground and aimed it at Haskell.

"It's over." Kearns' voice had an edge that Herron hadn't heard before. "We're going to all sit down, calmly, while I figure out how to contain the virus in this room."

"Contain it?" Haskell hissed. "I've put years of work into this exact moment and you're not going to fuck it up."

"Please!" Kearns begged, a last attempt at persuasion before she'd have to take him down. "Think about all the innocent people!"

"Nobody is innocent!" Haskell scoffed. "I was going to sit here with you until it was time to go into the city to finish my work, but now I think I'll just kill you both."

Herron flinched as Haskell fired again and grunted as the round hit him. His shoulder exploded in pain, then a second shot drew his eyes to Kearns. She'd fired at Haskell and her shot had been better. As Herron clenched his teeth against the agony in his shoulder, Haskell fell to the floor with a bloody mess where his face used to be.

"How the fuck did you get free?" Herron winced. Already blood from his wound had soaked his t-shirt and the pain was overwhelming. "Not that I'm complaining."

"I've always been able to dislocate my wrist. A bit of pressure and it pops right out. I used it to get out of the restraints." Kearns smiled briefly, then her eyes narrowed. "Now, given I just saved your life, can I trust you to give me time to sort out your wound and try to figure this out?"

"Sure." Herron lied. He needed to kill Kearns and then himself. If he could do it all inside the house, the virus wouldn't be eradicated, but its spread would be isolated. He could call the CDC before he put a gun to his own head, trusting they'd clean it up.

Kearns nodded, walked to the bench and returned with a scalpel. She cut at the restraints, sawing through them with the sharp blade. As soon as she was done, she backed away a little, her expression concerned. "It looks like you've got a pus—"

Herron struck like a viper. Despite the wound in his shoulder searing with pain, he lunged forward and gripped the pistol Kearns had placed on the floor after shooting Haskell. She let out a squeal as he aimed at her and picked up the other pistol off the ground. Less than three seconds after Kearns had freed him, he had a pair of weapons on her.

"You're an asshole!" Kearns sneered and her eyes filled with hatred. "I was trying to tell you that there's a pustule above the neckline of your t-shirt. The virus is starting to act."

"Then it's time for us all to die." Herron's voice was cold and detached. He'd already mentally untethered himself from Kearns and his own life.

"Listen to me!" Kearns held her hand out, gesturing at Haskell's body. "This is the lab of the man who planned all of this! Let me dress your wound and then call in the CDC."

Herron hesitated. Normally he'd have ended the threat already. Given he'd fought so hard and come so close to failing so many times, his reluctance to kill Erica Kearns surprised him. It spoke to how much she'd affected him in the past few days and how valuable her help had been that he was considering her request at all. Anyone else would be dead on the ground already.

"Please, Mitch, give me a chance." Kearns' voice cracked. "If we call in the CDC, we might be able to figure out another way."

"There's no other way." Herron half squeezed the trigger of the pistol and watched her eyes close...

A loud beep and a hiss came from behind him. Herron eased off on the trigger, but kept one pistol trained on Kearns as he half turned and aimed the other at the door. It opened automatically to reveal a little girl of about five. She was standing in her pyjamas and clutching a worn stuffed bunny, a look of tired confusion on her face.

"Daddy?" The girl's soft voice quivered as she locked eyes on her father's body, lying still, blood pooled around it. Her mouth fell open and she clutched the bunny tighter.

"Shit." Herron lowered the pistol and stepped between the girl and Haskell's corpse, blocking her view of her dead father. He turned to Kearns. "Look after her for a minute."

Herron and Kearns moved in unison, the scientist moving to take care of the girl while Herron grabbed a few blankets from one of the camp beds. He threw the covers over Haskell's body, arranging them with his toe so that his body was concealed and the blood soaked up. He'd missed the girl when he'd been searching the house and now she needed to die too; that didn't mean he should make it any more traumatic than he had to.

Satisfied he'd done the best he could to obscure the body, he turned back to Kearns and the girl, gripping the pistol tight. "It's time, Erica."

"Mitch, wait, look at her. She doesn't have pustules like us." Kearns hugged the girl tight. "I don't think she's infected. There might be a chance."

* * *

Herron still had a pistol aimed at Kearns. She'd dressed his wound and he was leaning against the wall, feeling weaker with each passing minute and unable to keep his thoughts straight. "Explain it to me one more time, Erica. Nice and simple."

"I don't think the girl is infected. If I'm right, either Haskell didn't inject her or there's a way to stop it." Kearns' was whispering. She clearly didn't want to upset the girl, who was seated on the other camp bed and clutching the bunny tight. "I just need ten minutes to figure out which."

Herron glanced at the clock on the wall and decided there was reason enough to give her that. He nodded and she got straight to work. He let her lance one of his lesions and extract the fluid inside, keeping the pistol trained on her the entire time. Then she did the same to one of her own lesions and walked both samples over to the lab equipment. It took her a few minutes to examine both samples, after which she looked at him and nodded.

"Both of us?" He raised an eyebrow at her.

"Yes." Her voice was grave. "Now I need to see if she has it or not."

"And if she does?"

She shrugged. "If she does, nothing has changed, you do... what you have to do. But if she doesn't..."

Herron nodded and watched Kearns work. She crouched down to the girl and whispered in her ear reassuringly as she took a blood sample. Then he glanced at the clock. Though he'd relented and given her a chance to crack the virus, he wouldn't give her a second more than the allocation of time they'd agreed.

"Five minutes down, Erica." His voice was laced with warning. "If you've got any genies to pull out of a bottle, I suggest you do it soon."

She didn't even acknowledge his words as she walked the girl's blood sample over to the lab equipment. A rash had formed on Kearns' body, more extensively than on his, another sign the virus was working faster than expected and there wasn't long to go. As far as he could see, there were still none on Haskell's daughter.

The seconds ticked by and Herron grew weaker. He was determined to give Kearns the exactly amount of time they'd agreed to, but he was deteriorating and he wasn't sure he'd last another five seconds, let alone five minutes. Though he wouldn't breach his commitment, he regretted relenting to her request at all. If he hadn't, both his life and his mission would be over by now.

Each second felt like a lifetime. Each minute felt like eternity.

Five minutes... Herron's right arm slumped again. He let it fall, but made sure he kept his grip on the pistol.

Four minutes...

Three minutes... his eyes closed and he drifted off for a few seconds. It took all his willpower to open them again. The girl was staring at him. Kearns was still working hard.

Two minutes...

One minute... Herron's chin dipped to his chest. Lifting it again was the hardest thing he'd ever done.

Herron opened his eyes and stared at Kearns. The clock had ticked past the promised ten minutes. "Erica, it's time. I can't risk waiting any longer."

"No! Please!" Though her voice was desperate, she didn't look up from the equipment she was using. "I just confirmed she doesn't have it. Let me figure this out."

"There's nothing to crack." Herron glanced over at the girl, who looked at him with wide eyes, clutching her bunny tight. "I'm sorry."

Herron pushed himself off the wall, keeping one pistol on Kearns and attempting to aim the other at the girl. His left arm didn't respond. Instead, he slumped to one knee. He blinked, nausea crashing over him in waves, desperately trying to regain his bearings and finish the job.

He forced himself to his feet, which only made things worse. He stumbled and collapsed to the ground entirely, then pushed himself up onto his side and raised his pistol at Kearns, who had left the equipment and was approaching him. She backed off, although the fear in her eyes had been replaced by utter pity.

"Mitch, you can't even stand." She stepped forward and helped him up onto the edge of the camp bed.

"This...changes...nothing."

"I'm going back to work. Shoot me if you want, but I'm going to figure this out." Kearns turned her back on him and walked back to the bench.

Herron gritted his teeth and lifted the pistol, but he couldn't bring himself to pull the trigger. He wouldn't shoot her in the back. Somehow, he'd keep going for another few minutes and give her the time to do her work.

She walked to the fridge and rummaged around inside. Then she gasped.

Herron could see right inside the fridge from

where he was sitting, but the beakers, stoppered test tubes and plastic bags full of blood that filled the appliance didn't excite him nearly as much as they did Kearns. The scientist stood back for a moment, as if in a trance, then she shook her head and started sorting through the contents of the fridge.

"It's here, Mitch!" After another second, she turned, clutching a test tube. "I'd bet my life."

"You're doing exactly that."

Kearns gripped the test tube and leaned down to the girl. "Can you tell me your name?" "Lucy."

"Yes!" Kearns punched the sky, then she turned to Herron and held out the test tube: Lucy was written on it. "Haskell made a vaccine for her! He didn't want his daughter to die!"

Herron hesitated. Of all the things he'd expected her to say, that wasn't one of them. "You said the Omega Strain couldn't be vaccinated against. Bouchard said it, too."

"We were wrong and he lied. Lucy has already been vaccinated, I'm sure of it. There's no other way she could avoid infection." She held up the vial. "This was his insurance policy."

"I can understand him wanting her to remain alive after others die." Herron frowned. "But I can't understand why he'd have another dose in the fridge. A vaccine after infection is useless."

"Not always." She shrugged. "Some pathogens can be combatted by a vaccine, even after infection. Rabies is the most well-known one. The only reason he'd have a second dose is if the Omega Strain is the same."

"It's a backup dose in case she somehow got infected?"

"Yep!" She beamed. "Hell, if it works, we're actually in a better position than if we simply eradicate all traces of the Omega Strain. It'll mean it can be stopped cold."

"Oka..." Herron's voice trailed off. "Exactly how many doses do you have in that test tube?"

"One dose. It's nearly empty." Kearns paused. "I might be able to stretch it to two. I think I can save both of us."

"Think." Herron repeated the word. "Is it risky, splitting the doses?"

Kearns shrugged. "The risk is worth it."

"Too great a chance..." Herron's voice trailed off. "Don't..."

"I can do it. It's—"

He cut her off with a shake of his head. "Get the girl out of here and vaccinate yourself."

Tears streaked down Kearns' cheeks and she hesitated for several moments. The only way he could accept her plan was if he was certain that she would be saved, and any dilution of the vaccine to provide for him would risk neither dose working. His mission would fail.

It wasn't until she reached down and kissed him on the forehead that he finally smiled at her. He knew that she'd do what needed to be done. She understood.

Herron kept his eyes open long enough to watch Kearns prepare the shot and jab herself in the deltoid muscle. Then she walked over to the little girl and held out a hand. The girl took it, fear and uncertainty in her eyes. Herron smiled at her and gave Kearns a nod. She nodded back... then they were gone and he was once again sealed in the lab. No doubt they'd be in quarantine within the hour, until they were sure Lucy didn't have the virus and Kearns was properly vaccinated.

Herron's mission was complete. He closed his eyes and smiled.

"149."

MORE FROM STEVE P. VINCENT

The Mitch Herron Series
The Omega Strain
The Shadow Enclave

The Jack Emery series
Fireplay
The Foundation
State of Emergency
Nations Divided
One Minute to Midnight

stevepvincent.com/books

ACKNOWLEDGMENTS

As always, the acknowledgements start (and could almost end) with my wife, Vanessa. She's my love, my friend, my confidant, my muse, my first reader, my last reader, my biggest fan and my toughest critic. Through a lot of lonely hours that go into bringing a book into the world, she's beside me the whole time.

Thumbs up, as always, to my trusty team of beta readers: Dave Sinclair, Andrew McLaughlin, Gerard Burg and Nathan M Farrugia. They help to attack the ridiculous at the root, so it doesn't sprout into a horrible weed. You'll notice Dave and Nathan also have books in the Murder and Mayhem box set with me, so you should check out their stuff.

I have the best team in the business at my back.

Thanks to Pete Kempshall for the edits, which are brutal and precise. Thanks to Stuart Bache and his team for the cover, which captures everything I wanted Mitch Herron to be.

Finally, and most importantly, thanks to you – the reader. New and old, it means a lot that you spend your time with my characters and their adventures.

ABOUT THE AUTHOR

Steve P. Vincent is the USA Today Bestselling Author of the Jack Emery and Mitch Herron conspiracy thriller series.

Steve has a degree in political science, a thesis on global terrorism, a decade as a policy advisor and training from the FBI and Australian Army in his conspiracy kit bag.

When he's not writing, Steve enjoys whisky, sports and travel.

You can contact Steve at:
stevepvincent.com
steve@stevepvincent.com

Made in the USA
Coppell, TX
01 February 2020

15246972R00095